We Were Kids:

Who Found Their Way, Through the Cosmos

BRINTON WOODALL

DEDICATION

This book is dedicated to all of those that follow the universe or something higher than themselves that believe nothing is at a loss. Sometimes things just come back in a different form than the way we envisioned it.

ACKNOWLEDGMENTS

I want to acknowledge the creator for giving me the guidance to know that I am the creator of my universe no matter what obstacles might be in my way

THE LAW OF VIBRATION

James Rose wakes up on a beautiful day. Stretching his arms as high as possible towards the ceiling, he opens the curtains with a swipe on his phone. The sun is already set high in the sky as he looks down at the polished wooden floor beaming back his reflection like a mirror on the ground. James smiles, grateful to be in a position to wake up every day like a king. The glory of the moment is short-lived as he realizes that he is late to watch his nephew. He rushes into the bathroom, washes his face, and brushes his teeth as fast as he can. He takes a moment to inspect his teeth and to make sure there's no crust by his eyes. He undresses out of his pajamas, puts on a navy-blue button-up and jeans, and rushes to his car sneakers in hand. He gets in, ties up the laces on his sneakers, and puts the car in drive. As James drives away from his plush condo in New York City, he looks out sparingly to admire the beautiful scenery of the leaves change.

Thirty minutes later James parked his car outside of his childhood home. Getting out of the car, his gaze falls to his next-door neighbor's house. He sees that the bones of the house look a bit warped indicating an extended period of negligence. The paint that used to be a beautiful Kentucky blue now looks washed out and dull. He smiles as he walks to the front of the house and knocks on the door. He takes in the images of his old neighborhood and reflects on the memories and bittersweet nostalgia that fill his spirit.

His younger sister Jasmine, now twenty-eight years old, opens the door. She gives James a big hug. James lets out a big smile, embraces the hug, and holds her tight, realizing now just how much he missed his sister.

"Hey, sis...where are mom and dad?"

James and Jasmine release from the hug as they both walk into the living room of the house. Jasmine and James sit on the couch. She straightens up the couch pillow as she speaks to James.

"They've been on a permanent vacation since retirement. They hardly ever come home these days. "

James smiles. "I thought that was the reason you moved back home. So, they could help you. Though they do deserve a good vacation."

Jasmine laughs, "I did too, but hey it helps me live here rent-free, so I'm not complaining. I'm actually thinking of buying the house next door." James gets up from the couch and looks up at the house next door again.

"Wait Ms. Sampson is moving?" he says

"No. Ms. Sampson died. Didn't Malika tell you?" Jasmine becomes visibly sad to be the bearer of this news as frown lines permeate her forehead.

James looks at his sister and shakes his head. He takes a deep breath as the memories of his childhood vanish right before his eyes with the thought of Malika selling the home.

James, "You know we haven't spoken in years."

"You still butthurt. That she didn't end up with you."

"No. I'm happy for her I'm sure she has a good life. She was always determined. She would have figured life out just as I have"

"Is that so?" Jasmine remarks sarcastically.

"Yea…I suggest looking for another home." James responds, ignoring his sister's comment. "The house from the outside looks like no one has cared for it in a long time. I can only imagine the issues inside the house. There are probably several issues with the bathroom. I guarantee there's at least some water damage there."

"Mold…" he continues, "you must double-check

for mold. Confirm if there's a heating and cooling system inside. How old is the tank for when you need to put oil in the house? These are just a few things that you should want to look out for."

"While I appreciate all your insights and concerns, the reasons you've pointed out are exactly why I'm choosing this house! I need something cheap, and I can always fix it up with my big brother. Besides, mom and dad are right next door so I'll have plenty of support raising Adam. You, dad, and I can fix the home one day at a time."

"Well, it looks like you've thought this through and don't need my help. I would advise you not to buy that house. But do as you wish."

"Well, I guess I should get out of here, huh? Thanks again for babysitting."

James smiles, gets up, and hugs Jasmine.

"He's my nephew. It's no trouble at all. We're going to have a blast."

"Great that means you don't need any money for him, right?"

Jasmine smiles while walking towards her room. She grabs all her belongings for her trip away with her friends. She opens her suitcase and looks at all the items that she wants to pack. The first items are her essentials she packed her toothbrush, deodorant, underwear, and panties.

After the essentials' Jasmine walks over to her closet and looks for a nice outfit for the night and possibly for tomorrow morning. She picks out a nice royal blue pencil skirt along with a black blouse.

She packs a pair of sweats for the ride home along with a simple white t-shirt for the morning. She packs a pair of shoes for the evening and keeps her always handy converse shoes as her everyday wear.

All packed up, Jasmine goes through a mental checklist to make sure she has everything covered. Once confirmed, she zips up her suitcase and brings it out to the front of the house where James is standing just looking around.

Jasmine receives a text message from her friend telling her she'll be outside in a few minutes. She turns to James, "Okay, thanks for watching Adam. I'll be back tomorrow." James' face begins to fill up with confusion. He was expecting this to be a day trip and almost loses his mind. He takes a few steps away from Jasmine, flabbergasted, and begins to look around nervously.

"What's wrong?" Jasmine asks calmly, noticing the reaction that her brother is having.

James looks at his sister as if she has a screw loose.

"What do you mean what's wrong? You know exactly what's wrong?"

"No, I don't. That's why I'm asking you what's wrong? I would like to know so I can understand what the true issue is?"

"When you asked me to watch Adam you didn't say this was an overnight trip! If you did, to be honest, I probably would have said no. I didn't bring any spare clothes." James

Begins to lose his cool, foam almost come out of

his mouth as if he just took a cyanide pill. He feels tricked and is irritated with the lack of information that was given to him.

"But you love me and were kind enough to say yes…I'm very grateful for that. Besides, you can rush home tomorrow, shower, and start your day like nothing ever happened. Also, you're so successful! Why don't you just pull out one of those credit cards, and swipe yourself some clothes?

"I have a business to run. You can't just spring these things up on me."

"You're the boss. Run it from your phone."

James completely speechless at this point manages a fake smile, walks over to the door, and opens it.

" I thought so too, at first…" Jasmine begins to clarify

"…but plans changed. I thought we were going to the casino in Queens, but apparently, it's going to be in Atlantic City."

"I knew you were up to no good. Have fun." James responds

Jasmine walks to her room and double-checks to make sure that she didn't miss anything. Living back with her parents makes her feel strange like she's a kid again. She closes her eyes and remembers her room when she was little, the room used to be a dull pink with an eggshell color roof. The shelves that used to have all of her stuffed teddy bears now hold all the clothes that don't fit in the closet. Jasmine walks back out to the living room.

"Seriously I appreciate this, you've no idea how much I needed this. Adam come here and say hi to your uncle. I'm leaving."

Adam, ten years old, is now in James's childhood bedroom. He lays flat on his stomach, head held upright by the palms of his hands, and watches early Saturday cartoons. He's enthralled by the cartoon character's spacious bedroom. It's so much bigger than what he has and imagines what his life would be like if his bedroom was that big, and how he could have a bigger bed and a greater television set. His daydream is interrupted by his mother's call.

Judging by the distance, he concludes that she is by the door and ready to leave. James walks out of his room and smiles when he sees his "cool" uncle.

Adam gives his mom a huge hug and tells her to have a good time. Jasmine looks her son in his eyes and gives Adam a doting kiss.

"Be good now" she says.

Jasmine holds her son's chin and pinches his cheeks. Adam playfully pushes his mom out of the house, anxious to hang out with his uncle.

"Hey, Uncle James."

James sees that his nephew still has crust in his eyes, "Hey, have you eaten yet?"

"Not yet. Mom said you were a better cook than her and that I should wait for you." "Usually, I would take pride in being better than your mother but not at a time like this. Let's see what we got."

James walks into the kitchen, opens the fridge, and sees that it's almost bare. He looks around and takes out eggs, cheese, and bacon.

"Eggs and bacon, huh? Is that okay with you?" He asks.

Adam nods his head in excitement. James grabs a pot and a bowl and begins to beat the eggs and sprinkle a bit of cheese. Adam enters the kitchen and stands a little bit behind him as he places the eggs in the buttery pan. James sees Adam observing him.

"Do you want to help?"

Adam treads away lightly and sits back down in the living room.

"I'll just wait over here. It's okay." He responds.

James continues to watch over the eggs that he just scrambled, as the bacon that is now in the pot begins to smell up the entire house.

"Did mom tell you that she's thinking about buying the house next door?" Adam shouts from the other room.

James hears the question and pauses. The breakfast is cooked. He plates the two dishes and walks them over to Adam.

James takes a seat and answers the initial question, "Yea, she told me this morning."

"Is the house even worth anything? It looks a little outdated." Adam replies.

"Well, the owner never really had any help. She lived with her daughter. The foundation of the home is solid though."

"Is it true that your first girlfriend lived in that house?"

"Who told you that?"

"I'm just telling you what my mom said to me. I just want to make sure she's telling me the truth, that's all."

James gets up and grabs two glasses and a carton of orange juice from the fridge. He walks back to the dining room and sits down next to Adam. They both begin to eat. As their meal is almost done, Adam breaks the silence. His works cut through the metronomic sound of the two boys chowing down. Adam's curiosity about the home next door and his uncle's love interest is clear for James to see.

"So, what happened? How did she become your girlfriend?" Adam adds extra emphasis on the word, so it gets on his uncle's nerves.

"It's not a very cool story, Adam. It's pretty whacked and not worth any of our time. You want to play video games or something instead?" James tries to appear cool. His childhood crush still makes him feel uncomfortable, especially since it ends with him having a big house, yet still single and alone.

"No!"

"You don't want to know this story. I'm telling you it's going to make you tired and sleepy even though you just woke up, trust me." James responds.

"Uncle James, it's just us. I really want to know."

"Your mom talks too much. You know more than you should know. Especially at your age. You know that?"

"I've been told that. My mom says it means that I'm inquisitive."

"Do you even know what that word means? Inquisitive?"

Adam chuckles, dropping his voice in an attempt to sound more mature than he is. "Well of course I do, Uncle James."

"What is it then?"

"When someone is like me, you know curious of one's nature?"

"An easier word that is more universal is nosey."

"Look uncle James, every good story has a love interest even in my video games I'm supposed to save a queen or princess in about 50% of the stories. Do I wish there were different objectives sometimes? Sure! But a lot of the stories deal with the same objectives. I can't really complain, so I just listen to the story and play the game. Besides this happened like what…40 years ago? It should not be a problem now to express yourself?"

James looks at Adam with his eyes squinted as if he wants to strangle him.

"First and foremost, age has nothing to do with it. I'm just not there yet and it's not that big of a deal. So if you want to laugh at my pain, go ahead." Adam interlocks his fingers, begging his now, "Come on Uncle James. Tell me how you met her? Would you rather I hang with you or play video games all day and let my inquisitive mind... go to mush?"

James smiles at Adam, "You too smart for your own good. Well…If you want to know I met her. when I was eleven...

LAW OF ATTRACTION

The Rose family parks their car in their driveway. They've just driven out to their new suburban home. James and Jasmine, eleven and nine respectively, live in a one-bedroom apartment.

They would spend their Saturdays getting into good trouble with their many cousins, and Sundays having dinner at their grandmother's house. The meal was always savory, like chicken pot pie, corn chowder, and biscuit and gravy with a piece of baked chicken on the side.

Those were James's favorite times, and, in an instant, it was all taken away when his father surprised the family with the news that they would be moving to a bigger home forty minutes outside of New York City.

James hated the idea of leaving but he didn't have a vote on what was happening. James' father grew up in a small town and wanted his kids to see the slow pace of small-town life.

What James remembers is his older cousin telling him before he got into the car.

"Your old friends will always be in your heart. Remember old friends are gold and the new ones are silver." Even as a child, James found his cousin's wisdom to be lacking.

James tried to interpret the statement the entire car ride. His cousin also told James, "As long as you keep them in your heart you will never forget them. "James thought about all this until the car came to a screeching halt. His dad looked in the back seat, beaming with excitement, only to find he was the only one who felt that way.

Now at their new home, there's something new for everyone. James, along with the entire family, gets out of the car and stretches his hands out wide. He pop's the trunk open, walks over to it, and grabs a box. Jasmine grabs a box as well. Jasmine repeats what she has heard many suburban families say when entering their new home. "Home sweet home."

James pouts as he gazes at his new house. It

has three bedrooms and one bathroom. No basement and grass that is as high as a Midwest cornfield. The house is a thousand square feet with a total lot size of ten thousand square feet. Looking out from a window into the backyard, James realizes that the friends he once had will not be around. He now ventures into this foreign neighborhood to make new friends.

Jasmine and James are looking around the house as their father, Jim, enters with multiple boxes.

"What you guys think?" Jim walks to the living room and unloads the boxes. He turns to his wife, Patricia, and kisses her.

"You think we're doing the right thing?" Patricia asks nervously.

Jim, confident in his decision, looks at Patricia

"We get to say we own a house. Have a share in the American dream."

Patricia looks at her kids go into their rooms, Jasmine is excited, and James not so much.

"I know. I just feel bad that our kids are going to miss their old friends."

"They'll make new ones."

"I know, but James just has been sad all day."

"He'll be fine."

"Eventually, I know…" she pauses. "I'm

going to go talk to him and try and cheer him up." Jim smiles and nods his head. Patricia walks to James's new bedroom that is already painted his favorite color: teal blue. James has two windows, one to the left of the home where he could look out to the front yard, and the other window is located to the back of the room a few inches from where his closet door is.

James puts items from a box away in his bedroom. He turns around and faces his mom.

"You can come in."

Patricia comes in and sits on the bottom of the bed. She looks at James inquisitively.

"How're you feeling?"

James even at a young age understands that having a house rather than an apartment is a big deal. He tries his best to say the right thing, but his tone lacks conviction and leaves the words that come out less than desirable.

"I'm okay," he says in a monotone voice.

The tone of his voice makes his mom want to be all mushy but knows that this was not the time to be overly sensitive.

"Just okay? You're not happy that you've your own room? I think that's pretty cool."

James sits down next to his mom on the bed. "It's cool…but it's not the city."

Patricia grabs her son by the chin.

"It's not supposed to be, sweetheart. You know your father has been saving for years to give you an opportunity at better schooling and seeing something besides the city. When I was your age, I didn't have my own room. I shared a bedroom smaller than this with all three of my sisters! If I was you, I would give this a shot because this is a better opportunity for you. We'll visit the city often, so you can hang out with your cousins and see some of your friends.

James gets up and opens another box for him to unpack,

"It's not the same."

"Listen, we moved so you can see something different and see what this has to offer. I want you to wake up and see the possibilities here. You shouldn't feel bad that your parents love you and are doing what they can to show you something different. Moving here is not saying you forget about where you come from but don't be afraid to see what this town has to offer. Do you understand?

James nods his head and puts another item away when he hears a basketball bouncing outside.

"You hear the ball bouncing. You and Jasmine should go outside and make friends with some of the kids." Suggests Patricia.

James walks over to Jasmine's room wondering if she wanted to join him outside. Not used to her brother asking her to tag along, she throws her Barbie on the bed and gets ready to go. They walk a few houses up the block where all the boys are playing basketball and the girls are jumping rope.

Jasmine walks up to the ladies and asks if she can jump. One of the girls offers her a spot.

Jasmine stands patiently taking in the rhythm of the girls' twirling the rope and jumps in once she's ready. She comes close to breaking the neighborhood record, or at least that's what she's told.

James stands next to the boys that play basketball, clears his voice to ensure he's heard over the sound of the ball bouncing, "Hey. Can I play?"

Malcolm, who is the same age as James, offers a handshake and introduces himself. Fourteen-year-old Billy interrupts the peaceful exchange,

"Nah. You can't play. We don't know you." Making sure everyone hears him.

James looks around confused, and says,

" I know. That's why I introduced myself."

Billy responds, ball still in hand, "if you want to play around here, you've to beat me first."

James, unfazed by the challenge, says,

"That won't be a problem. Check-up."

It's clear that Billy is the king of the court as all the other kids step away for the challenge to continue.

Malcolm moves out of the way and stands next to the girls who have also stopped jumping at this point. The game between James and Billy appears to have captured everyone's attention. Billy passes the ball to James's chest. James passes the ball back. Billy throws it towards James's head this time. James moves his head out of the way and catches the ball.

Billy, "Balls' checked punk! The game is seven."

James smiles at Billy's face. He shoots the ball over the taller Billy. The ball goes in through the net-less hoop. James looks at his sister and the girl next to her turns back to Billy and repeats the score, mockingly,

"One, Zip."

Billy thinks it's beginner's luck. He gets the ball from the hoop and passes it to James. James dribbles the ball once and shoots it into the hoop again. The score is now two, zero.

Billy grabs the ball and hits it in anger. The ball flies over everyone, out of view. James lifts his head and tracks the ball, the way an outfielder would in baseball, and catches it. He takes a deep breath to maintain his composure.

The ball is checked, again James dribbles the ball a few times with his right hand before he runs a little to his right and crosses the ball over to his left hand. He runs past Billy, gets to the basket, and lays up the ball. The score is now three to Zero.

James gets the ball again from Billy. Billy takes a step closer towards James, blocking his view of the hoop. The previous three times he scored, Jimmy had a clear view, but now he figures his best chance for a decent shot is to emulate the G.O.A.T Michael Jordan. He remembered that when Jordan was between a rock and a hard place, he would try his signature fadeaway. Of course, James would try not to have his tongue out.

He runs while dribbling the ball with his right hand to an angle where he can try and shoot the ball, does the fadeaway to make just enough room to shoot over Billy. The shot clunks off the rim.

Billy runs and grabs the ball as it rebounds. He brings the ball back to the top of the court, made with chalk and spray paint. Billy squares his body to the hoop and shoots the ball. He misses. James now retrieves the rebound, pulls it back out, and crosses Billy. His opponent slips and falls to the ground, holding his body up with his forearm. James capitalizes on this opportunity, runs back to the basket, and scores.

James smiles after he scores. Billy runs over and pushes James to the ground.

"What's wrong with you?" Yells James, now on the floor.

"What're you going to do about it."

James gets up fast and pushes Billy back. Billy swings, but James dodges the punch and hits him. Billy swings again, connecting with James' face this time. James gets on one knee and holds his mouth. As Billy loads up his entire fist to swing again, Malcolm runs over and holds Billy back from hitting James again.

Malcolm says to Billy, "Chill. Chill. It's just ball."

Billy shrugs Malcolm off him. "Get off me." He says as he walks away. Malika, the girl standing next to Jasmine, walks over to James and kneels to meet his eye-line. "Hey, you okay?" James looks at Malika, and although his eyes have shiner and he's a bit blurry from getting punched, he can still see how beautiful Malika is. With her clear black bronze skin as if she were dipped in rose gold, and how the sun reflects slightly off her skin to a younger James.

"Yea"

"You and your sister come with me." James and Jasmine walk with Malika and sit on her front step. She goes inside and comes back out with a plastic bag filled with ice.

"Here…"

James puts the ice on his lips for a few seconds then above the cut on his eye.

He thanks Malika, though he can barely make up a word, and gazes into her eyes.

She smiles, "You're welcome…"

James grabs the plate and silverware as he continues to explain the remainder of this childhood moment to his nephew. He walks into the kitchen.

"There she was. The cutest girl in the neighborhood saw me get my ass whooped."

"Hey Uncle James." Says Adam, with a grin.

"What's up?" James asks, curious to see where this is going.

"Language"

James laughs as he puts the dishes in the sink. He walks back to the dining room table and apologizes for his language. He then continues his story…

"My name is Malika by the way."

James checks his lip with his hand and puts the ice back on it. He offers his name in return. Malika looks up to see that the streetlights are on. That's the cue for everyone to go back home. Malika looks at James and Jasmine and says, "I have to get going."

James with his busted lip responds,

"Yea…we should go inside too. Thanks for the ice."

Jasmine says thanks as well. Malika smiles at both James and Jasmine as they walk to their house next door. "

"No problem!" Malika walks into her house. James stands still and watches. Jasmine notices and pushes his shoulders, gesturing him to continue walking.

Jasmine "Come on. She's never going to be into you." James smiles at Jasmine, "How do you know?"

"She just saw you get dropped come on!"

James tells his sister to shut up as he opens their front door so they both can enter the home.

Patricia sees James' busted lip and runs over to her son worriedly. She holds onto his face and examines it for more bruises.

"What happened!?" Patricia runs into the kitchen, wets a small rag, and brings it back to the living room to wipe off the blood on her son's face.

"It's nothing Mom, I'm fine." James tries to move away from the rag that is being forced in his face. Patricia gives Jasmine a stern look to see if she would crack and tell her what happened to James. Jasmine looks back at her mother and says, "What? James said it was nothing."

Patricia looks at Jasmine,

"If you want to go shopping tomorrow…I suggest you talk."

Jasmine looks at James' face without an ounce of remorse. "Sorry. James got hit by this big bully. I think his name is Billy. He's like twice James' size."

Patricia looks at the bruise again and says to James, "Let me see." James moves away from his mom and her coddling. James shows his lip completely without the ice covering most of the lip. "You see. It's nothing."

Patricia yells for Jim to come out into the living room and see what happened.

Jim walks out to the living room. "What's up?" Jim looks at his family and sees James' mouth in pain. "What happened?" Jim says to James.

James looks his dad in the eyes "Like I told mom, it's nothing." Jim looks at his daughter who cannot ever lie to him, especially when he gives her *the* look.

Jasmine quickly offers up the answer, "This kid…he's like twice his size."

"Which house does he live in?"

"He lives down the block. I saw the house he went into."

Jim looks at James. "You come with me." Jim smiles at Patricia and Jasmine. "We'll be back."
James and Jim exit the house. James tries to hold his father back. Jim continues to move forward no matter how hard James pushes back to try and stop his dad from going down the block.

"Dad, please!"

"There's no way I'm stopping. You should have kicked his ass."

"I'll do it next time."

"There won't be a next time. Sometimes you only have one shot to set the example. This is me setting the example. Just watch."

Jim shrugs James away from him as they both walk side by side to Billy's house. Jim knocks on the door. James waits off to the side. Billy opens the door.

Billy opens the door, and asks with an attitude "Yea?"

"Is your father home?"

"Why do you want to know?"

"Well, because you hit my kid. Is your dad home?"

"I'm the man of this house." Billy says with bravado and steps a foot closer to Jim.

"Is that so?" Billy says nothing and takes a step closer to Jim. Jim slaps Billy in the throat. He starts to gasp for air. Billy crouches down. Jim kneels and whispers in Billy's ear. "Well then, man to man. You ever touch my son again; I'll do more than just tap your throat."

Jim walks away from the house. James gazes back to see Billy. Billy is still trying to catch his breath. James looks back to see what's happening to Billy. Jim says to James, "Don't look back. Just keep walking back to the house.

James feels embarrassed that his father didn't leave the fight to him. Little did he know, his father had just set the tone in this matter, hoping that no one will ever feel comfortable harming him in their new neighborhood. Growing up here, Jim learned that they take kindness for weakness. Although he raised James to be kind, he believed that you've to be assertive sometimes and make sure no one bullies you.

James and Jim enter the house. Jim tells James to sit on the couch so he can talk to him.
Jim paces in the room until he finds the words, crouches down so he can be level with his son.

"At the end of the day. This town is just like the city. Just at a slower pace. Don't come here and think these kids are cool and soft. They are just as tough as the kids in the city." He says sternly.

"But isn't this a suburb?" He asks, perplexed.

"Only by landscape, not by economics. This is an all-black community that was red-lined. It's been underserved compared to other communities in the area. Do you know what red-lining is?"

"No."

Jim gets up from his crouch position and takes a seat next to James on the couch.

Redlining is when a loan or insurance to an individual in an area is deemed to be a poor or financial risk, because of the color of their skin. It's when banks only give loans to people of color in black neighborhoods. Real estate agents only show you homes in neighborhoods with people that look like you, and not what your pockets can afford, in a white town.

I wanted to move to a small town where you can wake up early morning and hear birds chirp. I wanted you to wake up and feel that anything is possible. Those are my dreams for you. But now, let me tell you about the reality of this town. This is a town where people will pray for you to show them a sign of weakness so they can take advantage of you." He pauses briefly.

"Listen son, at the end of the day it doesn't matter where you live. Until the mentality of people changes it will be like this practically anywhere you want to call home. You must fight and crawl to earn everything that this country claims can be yours. You will never be free until you free yourself. You understand what I'm trying to say?"

Jim touches the temple of James' head.

"I think so." He says, still puzzled.

"Every day you wake up you stay focused and do what you're supposed to do. You must outwork everyone. You cannot be just as good. If that is the case you will be my next-door neighbor, picking up a broom with me. Now get out of here enjoy your new room. I love you."

"Love you too." James walks out of the living room and goes to his bedroom. He unpacks another box and looks back out to the living room where his father stands. Jim Smiles as he sees his son enter his bedroom…

That summer James knew that he had to buy a computer. At his age, he wouldn't be able to get working papers that are needed to get a job at an establishment. He needed to find a way to make money so he could fund his computer and dream past his circumstances. James decided that he can do yard clean-ups, and knocked on every house possible asking if they wanted to use his service. He offered to clean up the yard by removing weeds or planting mulch before the next season in some neighbors' flower beds.

Of the neighbors that said yes to the potential service, he offered the older ones help with buying groceries.

Many of them gave him small things to do like meet them at the local grocery store, hold the grocery cart, go down all the isles, grab what they wanted, take it to their cart, and help them load it into their cars. He would then ride his bike back as fast as he could to their home and help move the groceries inside.

James even took on car washing for a few homes to earn some money. This job didn't please Jim as it was dependent on his supplies.

By the time summer was almost finished; James found his stride in balancing life as a kid in a new neighborhood and making money to help propel him to a better future.

The first day of school arrives. James packs his school bag and knocks on his sister's door. She opens the door and puts her book bag on her back.

As the two of them go to the front door Patricia runs into the room with a camera and tells them to stop where they are. They expected this and turn around reluctantly, forcing a smile. Patricia takes a picturing of the two smiling, and before she can cry James and Jasmine are already out of the house walking across to Malika's house.

James knocks on the door. Malika exits and closes the door behind her. She turns the key to lock the home securely.

Jasmine, Malika, and James start their walk down the block to the bus stop. James reminisces on the fun summer he just had. It was a summer where he truly got to feel like a kid. They played from sunup till sundown, stopping only when streetlights came to life. They would play manhunt and red light - green light. Occasionally they would have water balloon fights or play drip, drip dunk. You name the game and it was played that summer.

As they walk down to the bus stop Malika turns to him and asks, "How come you didn't hang out with us yesterday?"

"I was on the computer."

"Doing what?"

"Research on home ownership."

"You want to leave here already? You've only lived here for like a month."

"No. I want to own a home one day so I can sell it for more. I walked into my parents' room and saw them watching some T.V. show and I thought it was cool."

"So that's what you want to do when you grow up?"

"Yea, I'll start with homes and work my way to commercial real-estate." James, Malika, and Jasmine get to the bus stop. There James sees Malcolm and Billy.

Malika looks at James then at Malcolm and Billy.

"Hey, don't worry about him"

"I'm won't." The school bus arrives at the stop. All the kids get on the bus.

The school day was the same as all first school days, a simple introduction to the teacher followed by recalling the things everyone did over the summer. After school, they found their bus and headed back home.

The three get off the school bus and walk up the block to their house.

"I heard Ms. McGee is tough, from the students she had last year." Malika says.

"Really? She doesn't seem so bad." James

replies.

"I heard she's tough on grades. She's already given us homework for the week. Do you know how crazy that is?" Malika says, visibly stressed out from the first day of school.

"Hey, you want to come by for dinner? My mom is making chicken, with rice and beans, and probably a salad or frozen broccoli. One or the other…we can do our homework together?"

"I can't. My mom already cooked for me."

Jasmine runs into the house.

James forces a smile, trying his best to hide the disappointment.

"That's cool. Maybe next time."

James and Malika walk to their homes. Malika opens her door and enters to see a drunk-looking man hugged up with her mother.

The man touches her mother as he focuses his gaze on Malika. Malika nervously moves out of his sight into the kitchen, as fast as she can. She checks the fridge and sees there's no food. She then walks into her bedroom, grabs a pillow, and lays across her bed. She takes a deep breath and gets up from her bed, opens the door, rushes out of the house to James's house.

At the Rose family home, Patricia hears a knock at the door. Patricia, preoccupied in the kitchen, yells for James to get the door. James walks to the front door, opens it, and is surprised by Malika standing there.

"Oh. Hey."

"Hey. Uhm. Do you've room for one more?" James smiles.

"Yea, come on in and have a seat." Malika walks into the house and takes a seat on the couch. James walks to his room and comes back with a textbook and binder. He sits next to Malika and opens the binder.

He removes a piece of loose-leaf paper and hands it to Malika. He smiles and puts his textbook between the two.

A few hours after Malika and James finish their homework, the Rose's and Malika sit down to eat Patricia's famous Lasagna. As they eat their dinner, they have conversations about their first day of school and what they expect the school year to be like for each of them.

Malika has never been a part of a conversation like this. She thought only the families on sitcoms sit at a table to have dinner.

Malika realizes that this is what a family can be, and this is something she admired and would one day want to have of her own.

After dinner James is prepping to do the dishes when Jim tells him to walk Malika over to her house. James listens to his father and smiles at Malika as he opens the door for them both to walk out of the house.

James and Malika stroll by the basketball hoop outside. James grabs a basketball by the court and shoots. Malika grabs the ball out of the hoop and passes it to him.

James shoots the ball again. Malika repeats her task too.

"So what's happening?" James asks.

"What do you mean?" she asks, perplexed by the question."You're shooting and I'm grabbing the ball and passing it back."

"I mean what's happening in your house. You looked shaken when you came back to my place, after you said your mom had made dinner for you."

"Nothing much, everything's fine."

Malika passes the ball to James, who shoots the ball and makes it.

"You know if there's something wrong. You can tell me. You're my only friend here."
Malika grabs the ball and passes it to him again. James shoots and makes it again.

"I appreciate that. Maybe one day I'll tell you,

but I'll be okay." She responds.
Malika passes him the ball again, but instead of shooting it he just rolls the ball back towards Malika and onto the grass.

"You don't have to tell me, I already know."

"Know what?" The perplexed expression returns to her face.

"I know that you like me," James says with confidence.

"No. What makes you think that I like you?"

"I can give you a few reasons. First, you came by my house for dinner."

"You asked me to."

"But you said yes. You could have easily said no."
Malika rolls her eyes and says, "whatever."

James walks closer to Malika.

"Do you find me ugly?" James waits to hear an answer, but Malika instead repeats the question that he asked and waits for him to respond.

"No. I think you're cute." James says to Malika. Malika smiles, folds her arms "prove it then."

"How?"

Malika unfolds her hands, turns to James, and says, "Kiss me" James takes a deep breath and walks closer to Malika. They close their eyes and share an innocent kiss…

James and Adam sit on the couch about to play Adam's video game as he finishes telling the story of how he met the first girl he had a crush on.

"Although that was the first time we kissed. It was far from our last."

Adam says, "Well you can't stop the story there. What happened next?"

"Why would you want to know more? So, you can laugh at my pain? That's not cool."

"No, it's a good story so far. You should think about writing a book. Maybe a different topic than this one but I think you'll be good at it."

"Thanks, kid. I'll let you know if I ever decide to give that a shot. I'll tell you, but I'll leave some parts to your imagination. You're too young for the whole story…"

THE LAW OF ATTRACTION- X2

James and Malika, both seventeen now, are outside by the basketball hoop in their neighborhood. The two of them kiss and hold each other's hand as they say goodbye.

James, "Are you coming over?"

"Yea, if your family will have me." Malika responds.

"You've been coming to my house for dinner since we moved here, so you're practically part of the family." Malika smiles and James returns the smile along with a gaze as they enter James' house.

James uses his computer as Malika sits by his side. The door is open to make sure that James' mother can hear anything and everything going on in the room. Malika was curious about what James is doing on the computer since he seems to have zoned out and stopped talking mid-conversation.

Malika, "hey what're you doing?" James, engrossed in his computer doesn't even look at Malika. He continues to scroll and answers her question right before she became too annoyed by the silence.

"Looking up properties."

"Why?"

James stops scrolling, turns his chair, and faces Malika. He gazes into her eyes and says, "Just imagining what our lives would be like on the other side of town."

Malika sighs. She thinks about the scenery on the other side of town - the beautiful shops, the carefree energy of the wealthy - compared to their situation.

Malika smiles at James and hugs him. Her gaze falls to the computer screen and she sees the house James was looking at. "That would be nice, huh? A home on the other side of town must be triple of what our homes are worth."

"Check this out" James gestures to Jasmine as he flicks through the photos to reveal where the house is located. Malika can now see the whole house and comprehend what it would be like to have the opportunity to live in such a plush house. James becomes frustrated with himself, wishing that this house was not out of reach for his family.

"That house is like ten minutes from here. It's so big. It has six bedrooms and three baths."

Malika, growing enamored by the beauty of the home and how green their grass is, turns to James and says, "That home is breathtaking."

James focused on one day having a life of grandeur calmly holds onto Malika's hand and looks into her eyes, "I'll buy that house for us one day."

"You know how hard it'll be to get a job that pays well enough to live on and save the money needed to buy a house like that?"

"For you, I'll work every hour possible to bring you a home like this.

Malika hates when James says such things, as she feels undeserving of these kind words. Her mother's told her she'll end up just like her, so such things will not be possible. The thought of that happening fills her with dread.

So much so that she doesn't know how to accept a compliment without either rushing to give one back or standing there awkwardly not knowing how to receive it without feeling weird.

Malika pushes James' shoulder, then grabs his face so she can give him a peck on the cheek. Patricia knocks on the open door. "Hey, do you two want a snack?"

She knows full well that the two can eat a family out of a house. James smiles at his mom and says, "Yes, please."

Malika gives a more respectful yes referring to James' mother with her last name. "Yes, Mrs. Rose."

"I'll make you guys a grilled cheese sandwich. Come to the dining room table in a few."

"Thank you, Mrs. Rose." Malika chimes in.

Patricia smiles at Malika, "No Worries. You're family."

Patricia walks away from the room. James looks at Malika "You heard that? You're family." Malika smiles at James mockingly "No, I'm not."

"Why do you say that?" James asks quizzically.

"Well, because there's no ring on my finger." Malika flaunts her empty finger at James. He smiles and tries to bite it but Malika smiles and pushes him away.

James slides his chair closer to Malika and gestures her to come to him.

"Get away. You're nasty." Malika laughs hard.

A few minutes later Malika and James eat their grill cheese sandwiches at the dining room table.

"Mom! This is really good." James says as he takes the last bite of his sandwich. "Yes Ms. Rose, it's really good, thank you."

"You two are some hungry teenagers." Patricia walks out of the kitchen and into her bedroom. Malika finishes eating and wipes her mouth of any crumbs that might be left from the grilled cheese. Speaking in a lower tone to make sure that James' mother or sister doesn't hear her, she says "Hey. I have an idea."

James plays along lowering his tone too, "What?"

Malika looks at James and takes a deep breath before she expresses her idea, "What if we go check out our future house."

James gets excited, not sure if she really means what he thinks she means, "What do you mean?" James' demeanor exudes curiosity. "Let's go see the house that you were showing me on your computer. Are you down for that?"

James smiles and gets up from the dining room table, "I would love that, but we don't have money for a cab or anything."

"I know. Let's ride our bikes."

"I don't even know if my bike still works," James says to the idea.

"Well we won't know unless you check your bike."

James shrugs his shoulders, and tries to make sure that she really wants to ride their bikes to the other side of town, "You sure?"

Malika smiles, stands up from the dining room table, and gazes into his eyes and says, "Let's ride." She runs out of the house and James follows behind her.

Malika runs to the back of her house and grabs her pink mongoose bike as James goes into the shed in his backyard to grab his all-black Pacific Mountain bike.

They run to the front of their houses with their bikes and begin to ride out of their neighborhood.

Jasmine gazes outside her window to see Malika and James on their bikes. Malika waves her hand for her to join them. Jasmine just smiles and shakes her head to indicate no. Malika shrugs her shoulders in response as they both continue to ride their bikes.

Going through town, they decide instead to take the scenic route into the neighborhood of where the house is, rather than the fastest route.

As they ride James and Malika would challenge one another on their bike. Malika would get James' attention by riding with one hand for a little bit.

James, welcoming the competition, would ride his bike with no hands until they had to make a turn.

As they ride across the town, they see the stores that they've always wanted to go into but are steered away by the prices.

They ride through the small downtown area where they see all the boutique shops, the floral shop, Sal's Italian. They also see a well-known butcher where you can get fresh meats and a bunch of different eateries that James dreamt of trying some day.

As they approach their destination, Malika and James ride their bikes as slow as they can without losing momentum. They wish to relish the moment and see all the beautiful homes that appear to be massive compared to their own.

The streets are quiet and if you turn your head to the left you just see a beautiful lake with seagulls floating on top of the water. Two minutes later they reach their destination and see the big grand house that has six bedrooms and 3 baths. As they gaze at the house James and Malika speak to one another, admiring the size of the house, the beauty of the well-maintained lawn along with the flower bed, and how it looks nicer than every house that they've seen in this very rich and affluent neighborhood.

James turns to Malika now, "One day. I'm going to have keys to a house just like this for both of us.

"Really? How?" Malika asks,

"Hard work and savings. You ever heard of a book called the secret?"

"No, what's it about?"

"The book is about manifesting the things you want using a universal law that binds us all. They call it the law of attraction."

"What the hell is that?"

"Look. I don't know if it's true. But the law of attraction is like a philosophy. It states that positive or negative thoughts bring positive or negative experiences and things to one's life.

Malika, intrigued by the way James is explaining the theory from this book, asks enthusiastically "Really?"

James nods his head. "I mean that's what some believe."

"So how do we bring positive experiences? What do we have to do?"

"I like to close my eyes and picture what I

want to receive and do all that I can to hold onto that vision of myself having the object of my desire in my possession. Then take the time to write it out, and visualize it happening again."

"You never told me that this is something that you've done before."

"I know. I thought you would find it weird."

"Not at all, I'm actually very curious about it. What is something you've attracted?"

"I attracted you." James smiles and looks back out to view the house.

"No, you didn't. I just happened to live next door."

"Yes, I did. I knew the first time I saw you. You were cute then and knew I wanted to be your best friend. Now that I have accomplished that, the next step would be trying to attract this home for us.

"How can I help us get this home?" Malika says gesturing air quotes to James. James replies with a serious answer "You have to have the same thought as me." It's like when we go to church and all the members at the church do prayer wishes. The pastor asks the members of the church to pray for someone's health or a breakthrough, or for an abundance of blessings. It's the same thing here. It's just a focus between us and the universe."

"Oh. That makes sense. Show me what you would do to attract this house."

"Aright, look at the house and imagine us living in it. We're having a great time making our parents' favorite dishes while they visit us. Do you see that picture?"

Malika smiles with her eyes closed. "Yea"

"Now open your eyes and take a mental photo of the house."

Malika looks at the house.

"Now, with this memory locked in your mind, tell yourself that the house in front of you belongs to you."

Malika repeats what James said to her, "This house in front of me is mine. This house in front of me is mine."

"Now expect it and in due time. It will be ours." James says as he hugs Malika. They both kiss one another and gaze one last time at their dream home before they ride their bikes back to their actual home…

LAW OF CORRESPONDENCE

The next week, after school, the Rose family is having dinner along with Malika. As they eat their mother's spaghetti, Patricia decides to take control and interrupts the kids' side-conversation.

"I'm calling a family meeting."

Malika gets up to remove herself from the table, only to be stopped by Jim.

"Malika you're family. You can sit in on the conversation."

Malika smiles and sits back down, readjusting her seat back underneath the table, she begins to listen to Patricia.

"Your father and I are heading down to D.C. to see your aunt. I know you guys have school on Friday. I don't know if you want to come down with us or stay here. We'll be back on Sunday night or early that Monday morning.

Jasmine is eager to miss a day or two of school and therefore says without thought or hesitation, "I want to go with you guys. I haven't seen Aunt Ann in a while." Jim nods his head, not expecting it to be that easy. He then looks to the other kids and says,

"That's settled then. What about you?"

James did not fancy being stuck in the car with his family, knowing full well that his parents won't have the AC on, says

"I would like to stay here if that is okay with you guys."

Jim and Patricia look at one another before they answer James.

Jim thinks of a solution and says to James and Malika, "Okay. Maybe Malika's mom can come by from time to time. Keep tabs on James. I don't want you thinking you can have whoever you want in the house or have a party."

James, "Of course not, my mind is on the big exam on Friday. I can't miss it. Besides, you guys know me; I never go to any party."

"Better not be trying to have a party," Patricia says in a stern voice. She cannot fathom anything in her house getting broken or misplaced, all because her son wanted to be the popular kid for one weekend.

James, seeing the clear signs of reservation on his mom's face, tries to end the meeting by getting up and saying, "I guess we are good now?"

Malika follows James and gets up." My mom will check on him. I'll make sure I tell her tonight." She says reassuringly.

James, ready to leave the table grabs his plate and Malika's and goes towards the kitchen to put them in the sink. Jim, seeing no point in waiting around follows suit. He says to everyone "Now that it's settled, if you'll excuse me, I have some TV to watch." Jim gives his plate to James and walks into the bedroom.

Patricia goes into the kitchen and hands James her plate. As Malika listens on, Patricia says "since you are in the kitchen I would appreciate it if you can do the dishes."

Jasmine smiles as she puts her plate in the sink and walks into her bedroom.

James washes the dishes while Malika dries them. They're the only ones in the kitchen area. Malika is practically shaking with excitement. She's curious to see how James feels about the idea she has just had. She's not sure how to address it and is fearful of rejection.

"So, you're going to have the house all to yourself."

"Yea I guess so." James smiles as he passes Malika another dish to dry before placing it onto the rack.

"I think we should have a moment during the week, where we do something special."

"What do you have in mind?"

"We can lose something together."

James looks at Malika confused and turns off the water. Unable to make out what Malika is saying, he turns to her and folds his arm as if he's solving a hard math equation. He repeats her words. "We can lose something together…?" He says to himself, deep in thought.

Malika, fearful that he's speaking too loudly, turns the water back on and spurts it to full blast. "Why are you so loud!?"

James confused as to why she's making such a big deal out of this, turns the water off once again and says, "Why are you speaking in code?"

Malika turns the water on and whispers "I want us to have sex and lose our virginity together." James not sure if this is a great idea looks at Malika and says "Really?" to confirm that he is hearing what is coming out of her mouth correctly.

"Yes. We'll have your house to ourselves. We both know that my mom won't be checking on us. So, yea I think we should do it."

James, a bit nervous, feels his heart pounding. He had not thought of this and had just assumed that they would wait until they went off to college or something. The day seems to have come sooner than expected. James gazes at Malika, and although he is nervous, says, "Okay."

Malika, slightly offended by the unenthusiastic response, says, "That's all I get? I'm telling you that I want to have sex and your answer is 'okay'? This is so embarrassing."

Malika walks out of the kitchen but before she can get to the front door James stops her. He begins explaining his thoughts, without offending Malika.

"Malika. Of course, I want to have sex with you. I just want the moment to mean something and not be a disaster."

"It won't be a disaster. It's going to be great because it's you and me. So, Friday after school then?" Malika waits for an answer from James.

James thinks for a moment and says, "How about Saturday around the afternoon. My mom will be calling left and right on that Friday to make sure I'm not up to any mischief."

"Okay, Saturday it is then. Oh hey, don't forget to buy some condoms."
Malika and James both smile. They kiss one another good night. Malika leaves for her house as James watches out his window. She opens the front door to her house, waves at James, and disappears into the doorway…

Friday morning, James carries his mom's suitcase and places it in the back of the trunk. Jasmine hugs James and enters the car. Jim and Patricia stand outside the car next to James.

Jim gives James the stare of a man not wanting to be messed with. He says to James, "Now you know the rules."

James not wanting his parents to know his plans says, "Yes dad."

Patricia chimes in as she doesn't want anything to be broken or get a call from one of her neighbors, "No parties."

"Got it."

"Throw out the trash and do the yard for me since you're here." Jim says, smiling because he knows James hates to do yard work.

"I'll do the trash before I go to school, and I'll do the yard tomorrow."

"There's food for you in the fridge."

"There's money on the table, in case of there being an emergency. There better be none of those while we're away or we're going to have some serious problems." Patricia says as she hugs her son.

"There will be no problems." Assures James. Jim enters the driving side as Patricia enters the passenger side. James waves as his parents drive away.

James goes back inside to grab his book bag and to grab the trash and bring it outside as he heads towards the bus stop...

The next day, Malika wakes up to a loud knock on her bedroom door. Boom, boom, boom the sound rings out. Malika quickly sits up on her bed and looks out the corner of her window to view the front door. She's worried that the commotion could be the police. She gets up with an attitude and unlocks her door, screaming at her mom, "What the hell is wrong with you? It's nine in the morning on a Saturday. What's all the noise for?" Malika's mother appears to be out of it. Her hair is half branded, as she looks in different areas of the house trying to find something. Malika realizes her mother's state and is not sure what to say or how to communicate without her becoming more irate or erratic. She gently walks over to the couch lets out a yawn and says, "Mom what're you looking for how can I help?"

Her mother rushes over to her, completely off balance, and says louder than necessary. "Where the hell is my bottle? Did you take it over to that friend of yours next door?"

Malika, smelling all the liquor on her breath, answers calmly. "Did it occur to you that you might have drunk it all?"

Malika's mother grabs onto Malika's arm. Malika flings her tipsy mother off her and gets up out of her seat quickly.

"What's your problem? Don't touch me. You woke me up for no reason. I have no problem leaving you exactly where you stand if you ever touch me while you're drunk again."

"I wouldn't have touched you if I knew where the hell my bottle was." Malika's mother says, slurring her speech.

Malika looks around and finds an empty bottle in a matter of seconds. She walks over and grabs the empty bottle. "Is this what the hell you were looking for? Guess what mom? It's empty."

"It's because you and your friend took it. Thank you for proving my point! That is why you knew where it was immediately. You were trying to hide it from me."

"I didn't try to hide anything. There have been plenty of times when I've tried to stop you from drinking, and it's brought me nothing but pain and suffering. What was I thinking? I can't stop you from being a drunk. It's not in my power to do so, only you can do it mom. Only you can. The liquor store opens in two hours."

Malika walks back into her room and takes a deep breath, feeling much better having expressed herself. Despite that, a part of her wonders if she was too hard on her. Malika walks back into her bedroom. Her mother walks past the bedroom and into the bathroom. She looks at herself in the mirror and realizes that she no longer knows who she is. She turns on the faucet and splashes water onto her face…

James and Malcolm walk towards the gas station so James can buy a gallon of gas for his lawnmower.

"So, what are you going to get from the gas station?

"A gallon of gas for the lawnmower and some soda."

"Soda from the gas station? You'd be better served going to the supermarket. You don't have anything else to drink in the house?"

"I told you, I'm getting gas, and since I'm

there I might as well buy soda."

Malcolm looks at James and stops walking. "No, you're not. Keep it real with me. What are you getting?" James now seriously annoyed with Malcolm, keeps walking. Malcolm has to jog briefly to catch up to him. James gives Malcolm a serious look and says, "Look, if I tell you, you better keep your mouth shut."

"Of course! What kind of a friend do you think I am?"

"I take you as a friend who always says the wrong thing at the wrong time."

Malcolm stops, clearly unhappy with this characterization, he says to James "It happened once and now I'm known for that? Come on James, you know me better than that."

James and Malcolm stop in their tracks. James looks at Malcolm and says, "Okay. You promise to keep this to yourself?" "Yes." Responds Malcolm confidently.

James takes a deep breath whispers to Malcolm, "I'm going to buy some Condoms."

"What!?" "Say no more man!" Malcolm says as he does a gyrating dance in the air. James looks at his friend, shakes his head, and continues to walk towards the station.

As James is about to enter the gas station, Malcolm says to him obnoxiously, "Go handle your business big dog!! Roof!!"

Malcolm looks in from the window to see James buying the items from the gas station. James goes to the back and picks up a dollar soda. He walks up to the counter, looks up to see the variety of condoms and just points to the one he saw kids walk around with. He also puts five dollars down to pump gas.

James suspects the clerk is judging him over the one he picked. His nervousness fades when he realizes that all the awkwardness was built-up in his head. He imagined the guy laughing and giving him a talk about the responsibilities that come with his decision. However, none of that happened. It turned out to be a simple exchange with a pleasantry exchanged in the end.

James goes outside with a black bag and his gas container to fill up with gasoline. He turns his head to the left where he sees Malcolm gyrating as he pumps the five dollars' worth of gas into his container.

As James and Malcolm walk back to their neighborhood James is quiet while Malcolm continues to speak unnecessarily.

"Hey, hope you got the Magnum. Even if you cannot fit it she will be impressed. Trust me. I know."

James ignores what Malcolm says as they are back in the neighborhood.

Later that morning, James paces back and forth in the living room. He has already cleaned the house and cut the yard. To make sure everything is in order he turns the lights on and off.

"Ahh, it's too dark in here. It seems better suited for horror than romance." James turns the lights back on. He goes through his father's record collection and finds something that looks like it might be nice to listen to. He puts it on. The record is from the Jackson five, entitled the third album, and the first song is named "I'll be there."

However, unable to get the machine started, and afraid that he might scratch the record, he takes it off the record player. "How do you work this thing?" He says to himself as if someone can answer him. "What am I thinking? I don't even know how to start this damn machine."

James puts the records back into their box, and puts it back where he found it. He grabs a lighter and walks around the room to light the candles when he hears someone knocking on the door.

"Coming…" James looks around as he moves towards the door to see if all is in order. He opens the front door and sees that it's Malcolm at the door with a bag of chips.

"Yo, how's it going?"

James now completely frustrated with Malcolm, "What the hell are you doing here. It's going nowhere. Now leave."

Malcolm tries to come inside but James uses his forearm to keep him out of the house. Malcolm takes a step and tries to look inside the house.

"Is your girl here? I wanted to give you a few pointers. I don't want you looking like you don't know what you are doing out here."

"Get out of here before I punch you. Go home, have something to eat. Do anything but come here please!"

Malcolm, "Okay I see how you want to be. Malcolm smiles and walks away from James' house.

Malcolm and Malika cross paths as she walks up to James' house.

"Hey. What was that about?" Malika asks James as she's at the house. James kisses Malika on the cheek. He tells her, "That was nothing. He was trying to come by, but I had to tell him to try some other time. Come on in."

James steps aside and lets Malika walk in.

"So…you lit a few candles but kept the lights on?"

James scratches his head, not knowing what to say. "Yea, about that..."

Malika grins and taps James on the left side of his chest "Don't worry about it. I appreciate the effort." She says as she enters the home and sits on the couch.

"I'm blowing out these candles. Just in case, you know? Don't need firefighters coming to the house because I did something stupid. James smiles nervously and walks over to where he had the candles. He blows out all the candles that were in the living room. Once all the candles are blown out, he sits next to Malika on the couch.

The house is silent as they both look at each other, then turn away awkwardly.

"Can I, uhm, get something to drink?" Malika says, finally breaking the awkward silence.

"Yea, you want juice or water?"

"Water's fine."

James gets up from the couch, grabs a cup from the kitchen and pours water from the tap. He takes a deep breath and goes back to the couch and hands it to her. "Thanks." Malika trying to find a way to get things moving forward asks James if he would want to watch a movie in his room. She sips the water. James swallows his Adam's apple as this might be the moment. "Yea, we can do that. Let's do that. A movie is perfect."

Malika and Adam walk into his bedroom to reveal that he has lit candles there as well. James nervously blows out all the candles. He's too late though as one topples over and pours wax on his brand-new pair of new sneakers.

James moves fast to pick up the candle and then rushes to the bathroom and grabs a rag and pours water over the cloth and runs back to the bedroom to try and salvage the sneakers.

His valiant efforts are wasted, as he could not prevent the sneakers from the stains. He's not going to complain at the moment though.

James takes a deep breath and plops on his bed. Malika does the same. She settles in, and gets things started by cuddling onto his chest. They watch a movie that is already playing on TV. James smiles as looks in her direction. She gazes back with her hand and heads on his chest. She kisses him romantically.

They kiss over and over. Malika breathes heavy as James kisses her neck. Malika unbuttons her jeans.

James, not wanting to forget, reminds Malika, "I got a condom by the way." He reaches to put it on but is stopped by Malika. She continues to kiss him aggressively. "No. I don't want our first time to feel planned even though it is."

James looks Malika in the eyes to make sure she's okay with the decision, "You sure?"

Malika smiles at James, "Yea." James complies, moves his arm and throws away the condoms. Fifteen minutes after the act, with the box of condoms still untouched, they both look at one another. They have all their clothes back on now.

James wanting to be considerate asks Malika, "Are you okay with what just happened?" "Yeah" Malika reassures him. He can hear in her voice that she just wants a few more minutes of silence as they both take in this valuable and important moment.

But James can't help but ask Malika this important question that is pressing on his mind, "Malika, not to ruin the mood but I need to ask you this question."

Malika looks at James as he takes a moment to ask the question. "Do you think we should get a plan B pill?"

Malika rolls her eyes at James; you are ruining my mood now James. I think we are fine, and unless you have 50 dollars to go to the pharmacy, drop it."

"Okay, I won't ask again." They watch the rest of the movie that was playing. Malika sees the time and figures it's best to leave. Malika gets up from James's bed and says, "I'm going to go now."

James suggests that he walk her to her door. Malika doesn't think it's necessary, but James insists as he wants to show her a high level of care. He knows what they both did was a big deal as they were one another's first. James walks Malika to her front door where they immediately hear her mom yelling. She pauses for a moment, looks at James, and says, "Today was beautiful. Thank you."

James smiles and gives Malika another hug before she goes inside her home to deal with whatever demon her mom is facing today.

James walks across his yard, slowly, after a night filled with euphoric feelings. It was a step that he was not originally ready for, but at that moment he felt he understood life and had it all figured out…

THE LAW OF POLARITY

It's a serene Friday morning as Malika wakes up and stretches her arms wide. The sound of pots and pans being thrown around cuts through the beautiful chirping of the birds outside her window. Malika hopes this has nothing to do with her mom's quest for a new bottle. She gets up and walks towards the bathroom to freshen up.

After brushing her teeth and washing her face, Malika brushes her hair. She closes her eyes for a moment and slips into a daydream.

She imagines her house being cleaned down to a T as if she had paid for a professional cleaning service. She imagines her mom sitting down, relaxed, and unconcerned, completely disinterested in looking for a bottle, and waiting for Malika to sit next to her at the table.

Malika, well aware that today would not be that day, exits the bathroom, gets dressed, and moves towards the kitchen to grab some water. As she enters the kitchen, Malika sees that her mom has made her some scrambled eggs. The sight catches Malika off guard, and she looks at her mom in the kitchen.

"Morning mom," She says with a hesitant look on her face.

Malika's mother grabs a rag to clean the stove and responds, "The food's getting cold. Hurry up and eat."

Still somewhat puzzled at the sight of her mom cooking, Malika manages a smile. She grabs the plate of scrambled eggs and takes a seat. It's been a while since she's eaten food with her mom. Normally she would just eat at the Rose's home.

James and Malika both carry feelings of uneasiness, worried that their lives are going to change forever. They wonder if their parents would approve of them possibly having a baby. Perhaps they'd be chastised for letting hormones affect their decision-making. Both are deep in thought as Malika suddenly begins to feel sick.

Before reaching the bus stop, she pukes out the eggs she just ate. James witnesses the scene and asks if she's okay. Malika looks up after she catches her breath and says, "I think I need to take a test soon." James was not expecting those words and becomes quiet as Malika waits for an answer. The school bus arrives. James, "Let's talk about this when we come back home."

Malika, "There's nothing to talk about! We need to go to a pharmacy after school."

James nods his head as they sit together in the middle of the bus. Malika notices his nervousness and says, "Look, I might just have a small cold or something. It could honestly be nothing. I'll know for sure when I take the test and then we'll know what we have to do. We'll deal with it later, okay?"

James forces a smile and holds onto Malika's right hand. "We'll figure it out together, no matter what." They both smile at one another as their ride to school continues.

Later in the day, Malika sits on the toilet inside of her house nervously, consumed by anxiety about her future. She opens a brown paper bag to reveal the pregnancy test inside.

James sits outside on the step, nervous about what Malika is going through inside. He curses himself for not putting on a condom.

Malika gets the results and comes outside to sit on the steps with James. James hears the door open behind him and turns his head. He immediately offers his hand to Malika and pulls her next to him on the front step. Malika looks at James silently, and this makes James nervous.

"So, what does it say?"

Malika looks at James and tears begin to stream down her eyes. She tells him that she's pregnant. James, unsure of what else to do puts his arm around her. He smiles in reassurance, kisses her forehead, and says "We'll figure this out together. I'll start job hunting. I'm going to take care of us."

"Just don't tell your parents yet." Malika says.

"I won't," James comforts her with a hug.

Back at the Rose residence, James is sitting down with his family for dinner. He's eating his food slowly, in complete silence. He appears to be deep in thought. His parents notice their son's odd behavior, and grow curious about the reason. Patricia looks at James and finally breaks the silence.

"Hey sweetie…you seem a little down today. Are you okay?"

James tries to force a smile and tries to offer words of reassurance. However, he can hear his heart beating out of his chest before he can even open his mouth. His legs begin to shake underneath the table, and his eye begins to twitch. "I'm fine; I just have a lot on my mind because of college applications."

Jim looks at Patricia and holds the top of her hand to indicate that he would like to intervene. Patricia knows that her husband has a way with words and submits to his requests immediately. She loves when he talks to their kids.

Jim, "Son some things should not be stressed over. I saw you prepare for that test, and I know you did your best. You've taken so many other tough exams in your life, and you always do well. Just take a deep breath and know that everything will settle in your favor because you did the work."

James smiles at his parents and says, "Thank you. You guys are right. I should not be overreacting." He knows that if he truly took the time to tell them the entire truth about Malika's pregnancy, they too would become as nervous as he is. Though he hates keeping secrets from his parents, he reminds himself of his promise to Malika. As such, he knows he must always be a vault.

A few weeks later Malika is inside of a public clinic. She sits in the waiting room nervously, not sure if she has made the right decision coming here. She scans the room, gazing at the different people she's sharing the room with. She can't help but notice that they all appear to look like her: brown or dark-skinned. Each woman in here is waiting to see a doctor and talk about some of the options when it comes to their babies. The doctor's assistant holds a clipboard in her hand. She steps up and calls out a name. As she does this, a different set of doors opens to reveal a young lady about the same age as Malika.

The young lady runs as fast as she can to where her mother waits to hug and console her. Malika is nervous because she chose to do this alone. She lied to James and said that she was only going in for a routine checkup and would rather do this alone.

Malika enters through the big, wooden, double-door, and follows the nurse's assistant down the hall into a room where she is told to wait quietly for the doctor. Doctor Osaka enters the room shortly after.

Dr. Osaka appears to have a bright smile, and despite an obviously Japanese name appears to be African- American.

Dr. Osaka glances at her clipboard and acknowledges Malika with a handshake. She grabs a seat and maintains her characteristic smile as she speaks to Malika. "Are you sure you want to have an abortion? You've got other options if you're interested. Like adoption or keeping the baby now and giving it up later for adoption later. There are always families that want to have children but can't for whatever reason. You have a few more months to think about it."

Malika's demeanor becomes more serious as she says to Dr. Osaka, "I appreciate that you took out the time to share my options with me, but my mind is made up. I want the abortion."

Dr. Osaka, realizing that there's no changing her mind, decides to back off. She goes into a locked cupboard inside of the room and pulls out two pills. Then she goes into the refrigerator and grabs a bottle of water. She explains that Malika will feel some discomfort for a few days, especially during her next cycle. She assures her that excessive bleeding is normal.

Malika shakes the doctor's hand as she grabs the abortion pills and water bottle. The doctor takes Malika's leave as there are other patients to look after. In the blink of an eye, Malika takes the pills and downs them with water. Dr. Osaka is still in the hallway and Malika has already rushed through the process, run past her out of the double doors, and finally gone out of the facility. James is outside pacing frantically when his sight falls to Malika walking out of the clinic with her hands folded.

"Hey, how was the appointment with the doctor? Did they give you pre-natal vitamins and all that? You were inside for quite some time."

"No. I didn't get any vitamins."

"Why not?" James asks surprised. "You're pregnant. You took the pregnancy test two times they both said the same thing."

Malika refuses to look at James, which confuses him. Not sure what is happening, he looks at Malika with a look of confusion. He looks away from Malika then gazes back in her direction. "What do you mean no? What happened? You told me you were coming here to check on the baby. Did you have a miscarriage? I'm so sorry."

Malika looks at James with tears flowing out of her eyes profusely. "That's not how I lost the baby. James, I came here for an abortion."

James goes into a state of shock and begins to panic. "You did what!? Why would you not tell me?"

"It's my choice. I did what I had to do."

"It should have been our choice. I told you I would be there. We should have talked about it."

"We're doing it now."

"No, you decided without me."

Malika becomes quiet as if to say she's done with the conversation. James understands the signal and drops the issue for the time being. They take a cab back to their neighborhood. The car ride is silent, the air filled with tension that could not be cut with a steak knife.

They reach their destination and exit the vehicle. As the car disappears into the distance, they stand in the middle of the street where they shared their first kiss.

"You didn't tell me what you were doing about our baby," James argues.

"It's my body," Malika retorts.

"It should have been our decision regardless."

Malika suddenly screams at James, "You continue to harp on about that, but it's done now! Get it through your head!"

"So where do we go from here," James asks dejectedly.

"I think we both need time away from one another." Answers Malika.

"So, first you abort the baby, and now you're aborting me. Nice."

"I did what was best for both of us James! This lets you stay on track to get out of here and go to a school. I get to find a way away from my drunk ass mother. We both win. We don't have anything holding us back or tying us down anymore." James shakes his head in disbelief and walks to his house.

"We're just kids!" Malika screams as James pays her no mind and continues to talk. "We're just kids! We have our whole lives ahead of us."

James turns back around and enters his home.

Malika stands motionless in the middle of the street with her head in her hands…

Present-day Malika is twenty-nine and has a daughter named London who is ten years old. They are in her childhood home where Malika has just finished packing a box for them to take into their car. The two of them are wearing matching blue tracksuits, given to them for Christmas by Malika's best friend and London's godmother Noel.

There are several boxes inside the house, and Malika and London each bring out one to the car parked out in the street.

"Hey mom," London begins.

"Yea honey, what's up?"

"How come you never brought me here when Grandma was alive?" "Well. The timing was never really good. Your grandmother was a complicated woman. You do know what complicated means, right?"

"Like you and dads' relationship?"

Malika smiles in embarrassment. "Exactly, you know sometimes you are too smart for your own good."

Malika and London walk back inside to grab another packed box. "So, what was it like living here? Did you have a lot of friends? A boyfriend I should know about?" Malika rubs her daughter's shoulders and smiles. Her sights focus on the Rose's house.

"Yea, I had a little boyfriend when I was not much older than you. I was in high school. He was my next-door neighbor."

"Really? Tell me. Tell me." London jumps in excitement, wanting to hear about her mother's first love. They decide to take a small break on the steps.

"Well, I learned a lot from him. He taught me what I try to teach you. Like the power of positivity, and to speak for the things you want.

Stuff like that. His name was James, and we met when we were eleven years old. He lived right there. Malika points her finger in the direction of Rose's residence…

Malika reminisces about her childhood. Memories of when she was eleven years old, and the next-door neighbor kissed her flash before her eyes.

Malika and James kiss. They look at one another and take a step back. "I'm not sure what to say after that. Can I walk you to your step? It's getting late." Malika shrugs her shoulder in confusion. She turns around, looks at her house, then turns back to James.

"I guess. It's right there."

James escorts Malika to her front step as promised.

"Am I your first kiss?" she asks.

"Yea, why would you ask that?" he wonders.

"I ask because you're from the city. You move faster than us."

"Not by much. So, what happens now?"

"I don't know. Nothing, I guess. Maybe this can be our secret."

"You know. I don't have many friends or

secrets to keep. So, it'll be easy to keep this one." James smiles at Malika and offers his pinky. Malika smiles and locks her pinky with his. "I have friends but not a best one."

"I don't have one of those either."

"Good night James." Malika smiles and enters her home.

James stands by himself as the door closes, he smiles...

The next day Malika, James, and Jasmine share pleasant conversations as they walk home from school.

"Hey, do you want me to come by your house later for our history project?"

"No. It's probably best if I come to your house for the project."

"How come? We never get to go to your house?"

"It's just not a good idea."

"That's not a real reason but whatever."

"You want to know?"

"Yes. I want to know."

"My mother is usually upset whenever I come home. Sometimes she talks to me like she doesn't remember who I am. That's why I don't like having any of my friends over. I usually just clean up after. She's not a bad mother, but she is

not like Mrs. Rose. You know?"
Malika and James come to a halt right outside her house.

"Can I sit on your step with you?"

Malika nods her head in approval. James and Malika walk to her front steps and sit down. "When I wish to change something or make something happen for myself I write it in a book like this one." He reaches into his bag and pulls out a marble notebook. He hands it over to Malika.

"So how do you write in yours?"

"It depends. Just write what you feel. Write what you wish your life could be like and what you will do make it that way in the future. Write what you want to happen tomorrow, then next week, then when you get older. Just write for your future and take whatever steps you can to live it today. It sounds stupid but my mom taught me this when I moved here and thought I wouldn't have friends. As soon as I moved here, I got to know you."

James puts his pinky out. Malika smiles and puts her pinkie finger out as well. They lock fingers. James walks away and heads to his house. Malika goes into her book bag and grabs a pen. She opens the marble notebook to the first page and writes...

To whoever is supposed to read this, I ask that you provide me with happiness and allow me to be numb when my mother is under one of her spells. Allow me to feel loved by my mother when I walk into the house. I ask that you give me all the beautiful blessings that I see everyone else have. I'm not sure how this writing would get me what I want but I hope that it does. I feel better already, and I only wrote one paragraph. I'm scared. I sometimes don't see a way out and yet I dream to see one. I see the evils my mother is driven to because she's lonely. Help me find ways to avoid the pain or replace the pain with joy. Let tomorrow be a better day for me. Let tomorrow and the days after be filled with excitement and time spent with a true friend. Maybe my best friend, James Rose.

Malika catches herself smiling as she finishes writing. She puts the notebook and pen back in her bag and zips it. She gets up from the step, opens the door, and enters her home…

Presently Malika and London sit on the stoop. "That happened on this step right here?" "Are you guys still best friends?" London asks.

"You know. I'm not sure. I still think he's an awesome guy though."

"Why aren't you guys still friends then?"

"Things got really serious between us. He

was my first boyfriend and that changed everything. We kind of lost our way as friends at that point."

"Like you and dad."

"Kind of, but not really. It's hard to explain"

"Come on mom, tell me please!" London pleads to hear more about what happened between her and James."

"You're too young to hear this story."

"Tell me what you can. Please. Please." London smiles and waits eagerly for her mother's response.

"Okay...this is why you know too much. What would you like to know about me and James Rose?"

"Uhm. I want to know about the cutest date you went on, and the reason you broke up and stopped being best friends"

"It's a long story…you sure you want to hear this?"

"Yes."

"So, James and I are seventeen" ...

Malika and James sit on the step of her house. "How can we be dating if you don't take me out anywhere?" Malika says, half-teasing James. James cracks a sly smile and chuckles.

"We don't go anywhere because I don't have

money. Plus, you have to pay a tip. That brings the total even higher. I'll tell you what I'll do though."

"What's that?"

"My parents are going to be out the house visiting my grandparents in the city. Come back around seven and I'll do something nice for you that will feel just like a date."

"Seven o'clock?"

"Yes, seven. Now if you'll excuse me, I have some chores to do."

Malika smiles, gets up, and walks away. "Yes. Now keep going. There you go." James takes a deep breath and racks his brain to figure out a way to make the day special with a nice, planned date in just thirty dollars.

Malika enters her home and decides to clean up as everything looks disorderly. The couches are out of place. The sink is filled with dishes that she left spotless before going to school, but now look like they've been used to host a family of five.

Malika goes into the kitchen and turns on the water. As she washes the dishes her mom stumbles into the living room and says completely slurring her words, "What the hell are you doing?" "Don't you have somewhere else to be? You should go out and get me a new bottle."

Malika tries to keep her resolve and tries to finish washing the dishes.

"I'm not of age. Also, there was a moment when the bottle was not in your hand and it was a great morning."

"Well, I'm trying to make it a great night."

"Mom, do what you want. I'm going to straighten up and go to my room. Maybe you should do the same."

Malika's mother curses as she heads outside the house. Malika finishes the dishes, now completely drained emotionally because of this interaction. She can't believe she let herself get tricked into expecting anything different. The glimpse of what life could have been like with a sober mother, the way she was the day before, mocks her from her memory…

Later that day James goes into the family shed and pulls out a lawnmower. He lines it up across the house horizontally and cranks it three times. With the lawnmower running, James starts to cut the grass. The backyard takes him forty-five minutes to mow.

He then goes to the side of the house and grabs a broom. Broom in hand, he begins to brush the backyard patio. All this work leaves him completely sweaty as if he had just participated in P.E. for an entire school day.

James makes a call to the local Pizzeria and orders a pepperoni pie and an orange soda. After making the call, James looks at the time and sees that it's six-fifteen. He takes a quick shower and tries to look for the best button-up shirt that he owns.

He searches through his closet frantically and finds a blue button up- that doesn't have many wrinkles. He pairs the blue shirt with tan khaki's and walks out to his living room where he hears a knock at the door.

James opens the door, receives the pizza, and pays the delivery man. He goes out to the backyard where he pulls out a table and places it centered. He puts a white cloth over the table and places a candle on top.

James casts a glance at his yard. There's hardly any furniture but he closes his eyes to allow his imagination to make it the best evening Malika has ever had.

He runs back into the house and pulls the string that opens the ceiling hatch. From there he climbs up the ladder to the attic in search of Christmas lights.

There are many different lights upstairs, all placed in a highly organized manner. This comes as no surprise to him since his father treats the attic like a personal library.

James locates the white lights and believes they would look nice on the ground leading to the table. James also arranges the lights from the back door of the house to create a pathway for Malika to walk on till she reaches her seat. The backyard is now illuminated beautifully, radiating romance. He then goes into the linen closet and grabs a sheet with a lumberjack pattern. When he sees the pattern on the table he realizes that it's not as good as it can be and runs back into the linen closet to find a white cloth. He rushes back to exchange the clothes, and deems everything to be perfect once he does so. James takes a lighter and lights the candle. Malika walks to the backyard in a summer dress.

She is immediately amazed at how everything looks, "Wow. Oh my God. You've made it look so beautiful back here. James smiles at Malika's compliment. "I told you, I'd figure something out."

James walks over to the end of the table where Malika stands. He pulls out her chair for her. She sits down. He pushes her chair closer to the table. He grabs the pizza box and opens the bottle of soda. He pours it in the champagne glass.

Malika laughs at James and says in a funny voice, "How classy!" James chuckles in agreement, "I try."

Malika and James take a bite of the pizza. Her eyes roll back, wanting more of the delicious pizza. "Who do you think makes the pizza in New York so good?" James sits back and thinks for a moment, "I think it's the water."

"Really? The water?"

"Yea. It sounds crazy, but New York has the best tap water. We have the greatest filtration system in the country."

"That's something! I would have never thought of that." Malika looks at the pizza, and begins to gaze out into space. James notices this and becomes concerned.

"Earth to Malika. Hello. You there?"

Malika shakes her head and smiles "Sorry, just had something on my mind."

James holds Malika's hand and asks her, "What are you thinking about?"

"You promise you're not going to get mad at me?"

"Yea, now tell me."

"Okay so, my friend hasn't come to see me."

James becomes confused. "You have a friend that I don't know about?"

"Yea, I've got friends but that's not what I

mean. I'm talking about my friend" Malika says cryptically, adding extra emphasis to "friend". James still unable to understand moves his seat closer to the table and leans closer to Malika.

"I'm confused. What friend?"

Malika takes a deep breath and says, "My friend? The friend that comes to me once a month, do you get it?" James' eyes widen with shock and he says, "Oh. Yes, of course, your friend. So, what does it mean if it doesn't come? I kind of fell asleep during that health lesson." James gulps his soda. "It means I might be pregnant." James spits out the soda.

He coughs and catches his breath.

"Say what again?"

"I might be pregnant. Listen it's not for certain. I'm going to go to the pharmacy tomorrow and get a pregnancy test. Can you come with?"

James takes a deep breath and appears nonchalant. "I'm sure you're not pregnant, and yes. You are not alone. I got you. We'll go tomorrow and take you to your mom's house." James smiles at Malika. Malika returns the smile to James.

"James and Malika look at one another and brace themselves as they walk towards the pharmacy."

"You sure I have to come in?

Malika looks James in the eyes and says in a stern voice, "Yes. Come on."

"Fine."

James and Malika glance at one another quickly as they stand in front of the doors to the pharmacy. Once they enter, they look through all the isles till they find the tests. They go through the different brands of pregnancy tests.

"So does it matter which one you choose?" James asks plainly.

"I guess we should get the best one."

"I think you mean the most affordable one. They all do the same thing, right?" Malika shakes her head, grabs the test, and takes it to the counter to pay for it. They both walk out nervously and head out of the pharmacy…

Malika sits nervously on the toilet in her home. She sees the results, wraps the test in toilet paper, and puts it in her pocket. She stands up from the toilet seat and washes her hands. Then she splashes water on her face, looks herself in the mirror, and forces herself to smile. It's not good enough to mask the sadness. She collects herself and dries her face with a towel. She takes a deep breath and walks out of the bathroom and onto the steps where James waits...

THE LAW OF CAUSE AND EFFECT

James hears the door open behind him. Malika exits and sits next to him. She looks at James and tells him that she's pregnant. James consoles Malika and lets her know that he will be there for them no matter what. Malika asks for him not to tell his mother or father yet. He makes it clear to her that he will not.

James asks Malika, "Hey do you still write in a notebook like you did when we first became friends as kids?"

Malika not understanding why he's asking this all of a sudden, responds, "Occasionally. Why?"

"Good. So, when you get inside, I want you to write in your book and I'm going to write in mine." Malika is not interested but humors James and asks, "What are we to write?" James smiles and kisses her shoulder. We are going to write:

"Eleven months from now, *James Rose will buy us a foreclosed home that we can live in and take care of our baby. We will live in one room as he fixes the rest of the home up. We can do this. Please keep the baby."*

A few weeks later, Malika decides that she was going to get rid of the baby. After that decision, Malika was never the same. The loss of their baby caused a ripple effect between them so she decided to keep her distance from the Rose family.

Malika, who would usually be at the Rose family's house to avoid her mother, no longer has that blanket of security. To her surprise, she notices her mom is no longer irate all the time. Turns out she has stopped drinking. Malika misses the motherly instincts of Mrs. Rose and wishes to make a dish that would satisfy her mother. She hopes that Mrs. Rose would be proud if they were to ever have a conversation about her making Mrs. Rose's signature dish. Malika settles on Mrs. Rose's lasagna and garlic bread with melted mozzarella cheese. She notices that her mom is calmest when soft soothing music is playing. It helps silence the voices in her head, according to her mother. Light music from Frank Sinatra and Dean Martin.

Malika cleans the counter and lays out all the items for the recipe. Italian sausages, onions, garlic diced red peppers, tomatoes, tomato paste, dried oregano, bay leaf, sea salt, and freshly cracked black pepper.

Cheese, ricotta, freshly grated parmesan cheese, and a box of lasagna noodles. Malika starts to prep the meal by making the rich sauce. To do so she grounds the Italian sauce, and after being browned, removes the oils and adds the garlic pepper, diced roasted red peppers along with all the spices and herbs to create a bright red, rich sauce. As the sauce is about to finish, Malika grabs a baking pan from the cupboard and finds a smash bowl for where she mixes the Ricotta cheese with the parmesan cheese. Malika layers the lasagna with sauce, noodles, ricotta, and mozzarella. The second layer onto the pan is sauce noodles ricotta and mozzarella. The third layer is just sauce noodles and ricotta, while the final layer for the top is more meat sauce, noodles, and ricotta.

Once all the cheeses are mixed, Malika pours them onto the sauce and places the freshly boiled noodles on top of the baking dish. She waits patiently for the oven to reach 375. It takes around twelve to fifteen minutes until the oven is properly preheated.

The oven beeps to indicate that it is ready for the Lasagna. Malika places the pan inside the oven and sets the timer for an hour. She sits on a chair in the kitchen, observing her mom watch Jeopardy, and waits for the lasagna to cook. The episode ends just as the Lasagna is ready. Malika pulls it out of the oven, places the dish onto the stove, and cuts two big squares for the ladies. She takes out two plates and places one on each.

They both sit quietly in each other's company. Malika waits for her mom to eat and say something. Malika's mother examines the food then takes a bite. "You made this?"

Malika not sure if her mother is impressed or disgusted by the taste says, "Yes. Do you like it?"

"Yes, I do. It's delicious."

Malika smiles; happy that her mother finds the

dish delicious. Malika's mother notices her daughter's silence but feels like she has something to say. "I feel you want to ask me something. Do you?"

"How are you feeling since you've gone cold turkey?"

She smiles and says, "I feel okay. Every day is a battle. I feel a sharp pain at times on the left side of my body. I think I might need to go to a doctor soon. I don't think the pain is normal."

Malika holds her mom's hand and says with sincerity, "How can I help?"

"Do some research and find me a doctor that's good and accepts Medicaid."

"Alright, I'll get on that after dinner and see if we can find someone close as well. I think your license might have expired."

The two ladies share a laugh. "Hey mom, is it okay if I bring somebody over?"

"Who? James from next door?"

"No, I want to bring in someone else from the neighborhood."

"Sure as long as you clean up after and stay in the living room."

"Thanks." Malika takes the dishes and places them both into the sink. She puts the rest of the Lasagna into the fridge before retiring to bed…

Patricia is in the kitchen cooking dinner for the family. James enters the kitchen and looks at the food. He grabs a piece of chicken and nibbles.

"Dinner's not ready. Don't touch my food."

James smiles and grabs another piece.

Patricia glares at him mischievously.

"That's it," says Patricia.

James chuckles, "So…prom is coming up?"

"Did you ask a special somebody to go with you?"

"No. I don't think I'm going." James responds.

Patricia looks confused and says, "Why not?"

"I just feel like it's a waste of money."

"That's crap you should ask Malika."

"That's not a good idea."

"So what…you broke up? You can still go to the prom together. It's only a few hours." James looks at his mom and says, "I'll think about it."

"Okay. Get out of here. I'll call you to get a plate soon."

James walks out of the kitchen and into his bedroom. He lays down on his bed and gazes at the ceiling. He then turns his head over to the nightstand where he has a picture frame. He grabs it and admires the photo of him and Malika when they were younger.

James hears his sister Jasmine's voice yelling for him to come to the dining room table for dinner. He puts the photo back onto the nightstand and walks out of his bedroom. A week has passed, and the prom is right around the corner. James builds up the courage and asks Malika if she would like to go to prom with him. He figures the worst thing that she could say is no.

James gets up off his bed and looks at himself in the mirror to see how he's dressed before he goes out and approaches Malika. He walks out of the front door, through the grass, and onto the steps of Malika's house. He knocks on the door and waits for a response.

A Minute later Malika opens the door, with Billy right behind her. Billy gives James a smirk and tells Malika that he will see her tomorrow.

Malika smiles, trying to hide her nervousness about these two guys on her front step. Billy kisses Malika and bumps James with his shoulder as he leaves. James looks at Malika for a moment and turns his eyes to Billy.

"Is this really what you are doing?" Says James as he shifts his focus onto Malika once more.

"What the hell are you talking about?" Billy intervenes.

"I'm not talking to you. I'm talking to her?"

"You came up to my house. What's wrong with you?" Malika argues.

Meanwhile, Billy loses interest. He gets in his car and drives away.

"What's wrong with you? We break up for maybe a month and he's in your house. You've never let me in the house."

Malika lightly pushes James off the top step of her house. "First of all, what I do is no longer your business, ever. Why did you even knock on my door?"

"I was going to ask if you wanted to go to prom but it's clear that you've made up your mind."

Malika says, "Obviously you know my answer. What are you still doing here? You need to leave." James takes a few steps back, looks at Malika for a few moments in disbelief before he turns around and walks back to his house. He opens the door to his house, takes a deep breath, and enters his home. James slams the door behind him, almost breaking the hinges. Patricia is startled by the sudden sound as she sits at the dining room table.

"So, how did it go," Patricia asks hoping for good news.

"Yea, she has a date. I have a backup plan for prom."

"Really? Look at you." James forces a smile. His mom sees that his eyes show a sense of hurt and disappointment. James walks into his bedroom. Patricia gazes at the space that he just emptied. She takes a breath, and nods her head sadly as she continues to read her book…

The following week, prom is scheduled for the evening. James walks out of the bathroom, and into the living room in a tuxedo. Patricia and Jasmine who are waiting in the living room get excited. Patricia excitedly grabs her camera and snaps a photo of James.

"You don't have to do all that." James protests half-heartedly.

"Where is your date?" Jasmine asks.

"I'm meeting her at her place."

Patricia snaps a few more photos and says, "So I'm not going to be able to take photos with you and your date."

"No. But maybe her parents can give me a copy for you," James replies.

"Hmm…I guess that will have to work." Patricia says not trying to stress out James before such a big night.

"So, I'm going to go now."

"At least take a photo with me and your sister,"

Patricia requests.
Jasmine walks over to James and smiles for a photo. Patricia gives Jasmine as they switch positions. Jasmine takes a photo of Patricia and James.

James hears a horn outside and says, "That's Malcolm waiting for me. I'm going now. Love you guys."
Patricia and James walk out of the house. James enters the car and the two men drive away. Malcolm, also fully dressed for prom, turns to James and says, "You can find someone else at the prom and make her jealous."

"I don't care about that. She is long gone. I've never been to her house and the first one she lets in is Billy? It's over between us."

"I don't know what else you want me to say but what I do know is that I'm going to this prom so, where do you need me to drop you off."

"Just take me to the seven- eleven, and then to the park by the school."

"You're not going to prom?" Asks Malcolm.

"No." Answers James.

"Why not?" Presses Malcolm.

"I can't see her with my replacement bro."

"You can find someone else at the prom and make her even more jealous."

James and Malcolm look out of the car window. Malika and Billy were photographed by a group of friends outside his home. James becomes disappointed as he sees Malika in her prom dress.

"Please drive faster." James insists.

"Yea."

"Get me out of here." Malika sees James and the

pain in his eyes as he drives off. She elects to say nothing.

James sits on the boardwalk a few miles from the school. He hears the waves crash as he looks out to the ocean. He opens the six-pack of ginger beer.

"Can't get drunk off the ginger beer but the taste is so good," He mutters to himself. In moments like this…

Present-day:

London and Malika sit on the front step. They're surrounded by boxes as she tells the story of her first boyfriend. London is a bit more curious and asks about her dad.

"Well, London if I hadn't broken up with James, I don't know if I ever would have dated your father. He became my boyfriend around the time I was going to my prom. He took me as his date and one thing led to another. After a few weeks, I started to date your dad.

"Why did you guys break up?"

"We had a big fight. A really big fight," Replied Malika.

"Does he still live next door?"

"I don't think so kiddo. He went away for school and we never really saw each other again. Whenever I would see his sister Jasmine, I would ask how her mom and dad are doing. When it comes to James, I didn't want to know how he was doing."

London not understanding what the big deal about it all is asks, "But why?"

"Because I knew I hurt him. Although, now that I'm older I know that he would have stayed back and not followed his dream because of me. I know he loved me. He would have thrown it all away for me and I couldn't live with that. I'm sure he is doing something amazing with his life now."

"So, what was your dream mom? Did anyone hold you back?"

Malika smiles at London and says, "I'm living it. I get to have the greatest daughter. Come on. Let us get out of here."

Malika and London get up and walk towards her car. Meanwhile, Adam and James play video games inside. Adam beats his uncle and jumps up in excitement, "Finally. I beat uncle James." James and Adam laugh.

"That was luck," James says playfully to his nephew.

"Even if it was, I still beat you. Hey, Uncle James?"

"What's up?"

"I'm Hungry. Can we get some pizza?"

"Yea. I haven't had Albert's Pizza in years. Come on." James and Adam get up from their seats and walk out of the house. As they exit, James sees Malika. Malika and London close their car door. They hear the front door of the Rose family home close. As Adam locks the door, James stands still. He watches Malika through the window. Malika smiles and gazes in his direction through the car window.

"Mom is that him looking at us."

"Yea. It is."

Adam looks to see what his uncle is looking at and sees a woman in the other car.

"Hey, uncle James," he asks. "Why are you

looking at her? Is that Malika?"

James looks back at Adam and grins. "Yes, it is, and it's Ms. Malika to you. Hey listen, wait for me by the car. I'll be right back."

James walks over to Malika's car. Malika gets out of the car. They both hug one another and smile. Both of them are surprised by the randomness of them even spending a minute with one another. It seems like some form of divinity. It's immediately clear to both of them that they missed out on something special.

Malika breaks the silence and says, "How've you been?"

"I've been well. How about you?"

"I've been good."

"I was about to go get some pizza for me and my nephew. Would you like to?"

Malika and James hear the window of Malika's car go down. They both turn their heads down to hear, "We would love some pizza." London smiles and raises her window as she smiles at them.

Malika and James laugh, "I guess we've got our answer. I'll get the pizza."

Malika smiles at James and says, "Cool with me."

"I'll be right back." James yells for his nephew to get inside of the car and the two drive away…

THE LAW OF DIVINE ONENESS

James, Adams, London, and Malika sit at a table in the backyard. They're all stuffed, and there are only two slices left inside the box.

London excitedly sips her soda and says to the entire table, "This is the best pizza she has ever had."

Malika smiles, takes a napkin, and gently removes the tomato sauce that was left on the right side of her cheek. "Yes, it is. I can't believe it still tastes this good after all these years."

Adam looks at London, trying to think of a way to give the adults some time to themselves. "Hey, you want to play video games?" London looks at her mom hoping she says yes. Malika can't help but say yes as she smiles and plays with her daughter's head "That's up to Mr. James."

James smiles and says to London and Adam, "Yea go ahead. Not too long though. It's getting late." Adam and London enter the house. James and Malika look at one another and don't say a word. It was easier to speak when the kids were around, they both realize. There are so many things that they both want to say to one another, but they just continue to look at one another's eyes. They sip on their sodas, neither of them willing to break eye contact. Malika decides to break the ice, "Thank you for the pizza."

"No problem. So, what has been happening with you? How's life?

"Just life. Was packing some of my mom's stuff, trying to get it cleaned out and find a buyer. Your sister said that she might be interested." "Yea. I heard you're selling it. My condolences."

I appreciate that, but we both know how my mother was when we were younger. Although a few weeks after we split my mother got clean. Ultimately it was a bit too late. Her overindulgence led to her eventual demise. It became better towards the end. Billy helped me through her illness, and we even lived in his house for a few years until it was too much for me to keep up with. So now, we're going to sell it. How long are you in town for?"

"Until tomorrow. I was watching Adam for Jasmine. I assumed her trip was just for a few hours. Next thing you know I see her with an overnight bag."

James shakes his head as the two of them share a laugh. "Where'd she go?"

"Atlantic City."

"The last time we ate pizza together was what? Thirteen years ago? You remember the conversation?"

"Oh yea, the friendly conversation." James' tone becomes more serious. Malika becomes nervous and tries to laugh it off, but the only one giggling is her.

"Yea, that conversation."

"I remember the days after. I'm sorry for the way we fought. I should have been more understanding. You were right. We were kids. I had no right getting angry about what you choose to do with your body. Please forgive me."

"I appreciate that. At the end of the day, you weren't wrong for feeling as you did. I just knew at seventeen, I could not manage it. I apologize for not telling you. Even having my daughter at nineteen was early, especially with her father not being in the picture. Well, choosing not to be in the picture."

James becomes sad upon hearing her go through such tough times with a man. "I'm sorry to hear that."

"Don't be. I made the choice…hey, have you ever gone to the other side of town and check the home we rode to on our bikes when we were kids? I wonder who bought the house in the end.

"Yea. I'm the homeowner. Although there was a buyer beforehand my business manager suggested that it's a good opportunity to expand my real estate portfolio, so I bought the house."

"Wow. Really? Congratulations."

"Thank you. Jasmines in a similar boat as you. That's why I wanted to be closer to her and Adam. I plan on spending more time in that house very shortly. Just haven't had the time to pack up some things and furnish it."

"You've always been a sweet guy. It doesn't surprise me at all that you want to be there to support Jasmine and Adam."

"I appreciate that. Now that we've apologized, and since we're no longer kids, can I take you out to eat without any kids?"

Malika surprised by James' candor nods her head, almost stuttering on her words. She finally takes a deep breath and says, "If you can find me a babysitter. Sure. I would love that."

"Yea. We can figure something out. I'll have Jasmine watch London if we must. She owes me, and London can hang out with Adam."

Malika likes the idea. "Okay, I'm down. When?"

"Can you do tomorrow?" James asks hoping she says yes. She insists that she's down for the date but needs some time to think of a day. James and Malika enter the house where they all say good night to one another. London and Malika leave the Rose family home and drive to their apartment a few towns away.

They enter their apartment and carry two boxes into the house. Malika tells London to wash up and get ready for bed. As London does what her mother tells her. Malika looks at her phone and calls James as she cannot get him off her mind…

James is in the living room where Adam sits exhausted. He wishes his uncle a good night and walks into the bedroom. James feels his phone vibrate. He doesn't recognize the number and answers, "Hey it's me," Says Malika on the other end.

James is shocked to hear from Malika

already. He smiles and traps the phone comfortably between his shoulder and his cheek. "Hi. So, did you make a decision?"

"I did. My answer is yes. Tomorrow will be fine. Since it's a school night I'm going to see if my friend can watch her instead. If she's unavailable and can you ask Jasmine? I'll appreciate it."

"That should work. She does owe me so whether I cash in this favor now or later it's all good with me. What time works for you?"

Malika thinks about it for a moment and decides on the time, "How about six o'clock? Does that work for you?"

"Just being able to spend time with you will always work for me. Six o'clock sounds great." Malika smiles and wishes James a good night…

The next morning James wakes up to Adam trying to sneakily play video games on the same couch that James was sleeping on. James looks at his nephew and cannot help but feel joy when he sees him do the same thing he would do as a kid. Playing video games early in the day on the weekend is a great strategy. It gives you plenty of time before you're told to do a chore or something of that sort. "Hey what are you doing?"

Adam focuses on the video game, glances at his uncle, and says, "Getting my skills up to beat you again." James sits up from the couch "Is that right? I guess I'll have to show you who the boss is." James gets up and grabs the second controller, puts himself in the game, and the two play for three hours straight until they both hear a car stop outside of their house.

They both turn their heads to see who it might be. The door opens to reveal that it's Adam's mother with her duffle bag. She walks to the house and before she can open the door for herself, James opens the door and helps her with her duffle bag, taking it off her shoulder and rushing to put it in her room.

Jasmine is surprised to see James in such a rush to grab her duffle bag. James grabs anything she might have come with and says, "Hey. Love you."

Jasmine expecting to spend some time with her brother, asks, "Where are you going?" "Out?" he responds.

Jasmine smiles, wanting more information, "Yea but with whom?"

James responds nonchalantly, hiding his excitement, "I'm supposed to go out with Malika." Jasmine becomes excited for James, "What no...did I hear the name that I think I just heard?"

"Yes, you did, and I need to go home and shower and find something to wear. I'm running late." James hugs his nephew as he exits through the front door. Jasmine screams out to James as the doors close behind him. "Don't mess this up!!" Jasmine walks towards the couch and grabs a seat, happy for her brother…

Malika's friend and babysitter Noel listens to the radio as she preps meatballs with London in the kitchen. Malika walks out with two outfits in her hand.

"Hey Noel, what should I wear?"
Noel puts her index finger over her mouth and shushes Malika. "Quiet. This is our song, right?" Noel laughs and looks at London with amusement. London laughs as the two dance to the song on the radio while they continue to make meatballs.

Malika looks at London and Noel, "Come on guys, seriously, which one?" Malika insists, wanting an opinion.

"Go with whichever one makes you feel good? Sorry."

"Just help me pick one." Noel holds the blue and black dresses in her hands. "That black dress looks like you're going to a funeral. Go with the other one."

Malika looks at London to see if she has a different opinion "I like the one that Aunt Noel recommended."

"See? I know what's best."

"I've never asked you about an outfit ever," Malika says with a smirk on her face, shaking her head as she walks away from the kitchen. London and Noel put the meatballs in the oven.

A few minutes later Malika comes out all dressed up to see what Noel and London think about her outfit. London looks at her mother in awe. She has never seen her look so beautiful.

"You look amazing mom."

Malika smiles at her daughter and says as she feels herself now that her daughter finds her beautiful, "Thank you, honey." Malika, London, and Noel hear a knock on the front door. Malika nervously says, "That must be him." She begins walking towards the door but Noel grabs her by the arm. "Hey. What are you doing?" She whispers.

"I'm getting the door, what does it look like?"

"No. That's going to make you look thirsty. I've got it." Noel says as she holds her shoulders before shooing her back into the bedroom.

"Not with your unwashed meatball hands

you haven't." Malika inspects her shoulders and goes into the kitchen to wash her shoulders with soap. London seeing this whole scene unfold washes her hand quickly and runs out of the kitchen. "I'll do it. I washed my hands."

Malika goes to the couch and sits down. Noel runs back into the kitchen. London opens the door to see James smiling at her. "Hey London, it's really nice to see you again."

"Hey, James. You can come in. My mom is excited." James blushes, "Well she's not the only one. So am I."

London steps aside. James enters and sees Malika on the couch. James forgets how to speak for a moment, gathers his composure, and says, "Wow. You look amazing."

Noel says, "Thank you" as she tries to be funny. James doesn't even notice as his eyes are solely fixed upon Malika. Malika not finding it to be funny at all says, "He was talking to me. Don't mind her. She plays too much."

"I barely knew anyone else was in the room. Should we go?" responds James.

Malika smiles and walks over to London and kisses her on the cheek. She tells her to be good. Malika and James leave her apartment for their date...

LAW OF RHYTHM

On their drive into the city, both James and Malika sit quietly. The smooth rhythm and blues from their teenage years is playing on the radio. James looks over to Malika and asks her, "So tell me about your daughter, she looks like a spitting image of you when you were her age?"

"Yea she does. My mother, before she passed, would say that all the time. London is smart and very inquisitive. Sometimes I worry she knows a bit too much for her age."

"I'm learning that with my nephew. They mature faster than I could ever have anticipated. I do suppose we grew up quicker than our parents would've wanted us to." Twenty minutes later, James and Malika walk, slowly taking in the New York City skyline.

Although they walk down a quiet block, the city is still buzzing rampantly. Not for these two though. For them, the city seems to have slowed down, as if they were meditating. As they walk, nothing seems to faze them, not even the less fortunate that stumble at their feet asking for a dollar.

Malika looks at James and says, "What did you bring me into New York City for?" James holds onto Malika's hand as she readjusts to put her arm inside of his. "It's a surprise."

"I hope it's a good one."

"I think you'll like it." Malika continues to gaze in James' direction as they make it to his New York City loft.

The loft is plush. You cannot find anything that would appear out of place. Everything is precise and pristine, from the cherry wood floors, to the expensive couch that was shipped from Italy, to the view of the flat iron building from his window.

Malika and James drink a glass of wine as a chef is in the kitchen. "So, you've got a personal chef?"

"I wouldn't say I have a Personal Chef. I only call him on special occasions."

"So, this is a special occasion?"

"There was never a moment I spent with you,

that I did not count myself fortunate. Now that I have the chance to do it again, a day like this is bound to feel special."

"So, what do you have planned with this place? Now that you have another house outside of the city."

"I plan on keeping this one. Maybe I'll rent it out as an Air BnB or something." Malika nods her head to appreciate the idea. "I'm impressed, Mr. Rose."

"Thank you."

The chef walks over to Malika and James. "Good evening Mr. Rose and Mrs. Sanders."

"Look at that. You told him my name." Malika says with a smile.

James grins, "Yes. Now we can listen. Chef as you were saying."

The chef smiles at Malika and James and clears his throat to announce the menu, "Tonight, I've prepared a Braised short rib with asparagus and Mashed potatoes." Malika, excited at the options, says to James, "That sounds very delicious."

"Thank you, Chef." James says to the chef, dismissing him. The chef bows his head. He then inquires about the table's wine preference.

"I'll leave that to the lady of the evening." Says James.

"Red will do nicely. Thank you."

The Chef smiles as he walks away. The conversations of the night revolve around their childhood and all the things they did as kids. It was a delight for them both to catch up even more and recant stories that they thought that they had forgotten but learned that they hadn't.

Malika and James take a final bite of their meals. "This was so good," Malika says as she wipes any potential crust off her face. James takes a sip of his wine and wipes his mouth. He calls the Chef over and thanks him for the meal. The chef smiles and puts his hand on his heart. He asks the two if they would like dessert. Malika not expecting dessert, says with excitement, "Really? Dessert!?" She realizes how childish she must look, and feels embarrassed.

James smiles and says, "I bought pound cake and Haagen- Dazs. Malika not wanting to be wooed with fancy dessert is excited James didn't offer a soufflé or something complicated. "Even better," She remarks.

James walks over to the Kitchen, grabs two bowls, cuts two pieces of cake, goes into his freezer to retrieve the vanilla ice cream, and places two scoops in each bowl. He walks it over to Malika and re-takes his seat.

"Here you go."

"Thank you." They both bite into their desert, unable to take their eyes off of each other in the fear that this is all just a dream. Malika puts her spoon down and says to James, "Can I ask you a question?"

"Yeah sure."

"Do you think your life would have turned out different if I had kept the baby when we were together?"

"Like us?"

"Yea I've always wondered the same. I have never had a relationship like the one I had with you, as crazy as those sounds."

"It doesn't sound crazy at all."

"I didn't think my first boyfriend would be everything. James, you were the most caring and compassionate guy I have ever been with. I wish I would have known myself a little better."

"We can't live in the past. I'm just grateful that somehow, we at least got to have this moment."

Malika smiles at how sweet James is, "Me too. So, what does it mean for us now though?"

"I don't know. But I know one thing is certain."

"What's that?"

"We're not kids anymore."

Malika takes three steps to be as close as she can to James and touches his chest. She tilts her head sideways, wanting to be kissed. James sees the cue and takes a step closer. Malika moves her head closer to James. They kiss one another. James holds onto the back of her neck gently. They both smile as they gaze into each other's eyes. Malika feeling that this is going towards something more than just an innocent kiss, waves away all the little cupid's that are throwing their arrows at her, and says to James, "I think I should go home."

James not wanting to ruin the night and following Malika's lead says, "No problem." They walk out of his loft to his car, so he can drive her home…

James is driving Malika back home. As he drives, music from the radio fills the car, and both think about the great evening that they've just had. It has been amazing fun after not talking for so many years.

Although both of their lives took different turns, they remember the times when they were aligned and everything and anything seemed possible. That is what kept both of them going no matter what was happening in their lives.

James parks the car outside of Malika's

apartment. He gets out, walks towards the passenger side door, and opens it for her. This was a display of chivalry that she was not accustomed to.

Her smile towards James quickly turns to a frown as she sees a tall man standing outside her house. James notices the frown, as Malika thinking she's whispering says loud enough for James to hear. "What the hell is he doing here?"

Malika closes the door and rushes to her apartment door. James is still not sure if he knows the guy, but follows her just in case. As they get closer to Malika's door, James realizes that the tall stranger is Billy. Malika repeats what she had said a few hundred feet away. "What the hell are you doing here?"

"Who the hell are you with?" says Billy angrily.

"We're not together. That was your decision. So, it's none of your business."

Malika tries to walk past Billy to her door when he grabs her by the arm. James removes Billy's hand off of Malika.

"Get your hands off me!" Malika yells. James steps in front of Malika as both men face-off, and stare into each other's eyes. James asks if Malika is okay as he keeps his eyes on Billy.

Billy smirks, "She'll be fine. She likes it rough."

"I'm speaking to Malika. Malika, you good?" James asks, ignoring Billy.

Billy looks at the two and says, "Let me talk to my family in peace."

James can no longer ignore what Billy had said. The realization that London was their child stings him right in the heart. It's as if cupid didn't hit him with a loving arrow but a damn taser and told him to suck it up.

"Wait. Billy is London's father?" James asks Malika, needing to hear it from her and no one else. James looks at Malika, waiting for an answer. She just continues to look at him blankly, as he waits for an answer. Malika can see the obvious pain on James' face.

James shrugs his shoulders, and says, "Don't worry about it. I got my answer."

James walks back to his car. Malika and Billy look at each other as they hear James drive off in his car.

Malika embarrassed and frustrated at this point, asks Billy pointedly, "What are you doing here?"

Billy smiles and tries to embrace her by holding onto her shoulders. Malika removes his hands. Billy persists, and says sincerely, "I want you back."

"What about your daughter?"

"Of course, I want to be with my daughter. But I also want you and me to be together."

"So how are we going to make this work?"

"I should be the one questioning you talking to that chump."

Billy's words make Malika's head spin. She can't believe that he's making it all out to be her fault.

"You left me for some other woman. You haven't spoken to me in years. You didn't do a thing to help me raise London. I mean nothing!"

Billy asks Malika to listen to him as he tries to make his point. Malika, not wanting to hear it, wants to get her point across equally. She yells, "No! You listen. There's nothing for us to be. You left our daughter to be raised by me alone and now you want to come by and act as if we can be a thing. You are so selfish. You were selfish when we were kids and are even more so as an adult."

Billy takes a deep breath and against the apartment building. He adopts a cool attitude, and says, "Look I want you, but if you keep talking back to me with all this attitude, this isn't going to work. Think about it. Unless you're into that weak-ass punk you just rolled up here with. I know you'll make the right decision you always do."

London opens the door and comes outside of the apartment in her pajamas. London becomes excited when she sees her father, "Dad, is that you?"

Billy turns to his daughter and smiles. He gets down on one knee to be around her height. "Come here. Hug daddy." Billy has his arms stretched out as he waits for London to run into his chest. London leaps towards her dad but Malika gets between the two. She says, "London baby, go back inside. You'll see your father another time."

London stands there idly, not wanting to go. "No. I want to see daddy!"

"No."

"Daddy!" London yells, wanting to be with her dad. Malika yanks London as she opens the door, "I said another time! No!" London tries to stand her ground, but Malika grabs her by the hand and drags her inside.

"Don't worry baby. I'll see you soon." Yells Billy, as the door slams shut in his face. Billy walks away from the house with a grin on his face to hide the fact that he was disturbed to see the woman that has his child, hang out with someone who he's seen as a punk his entire childhood. He remembers how James' father came knocking at his door and slapped him in his throat. Billy hopes that his sight breaks James' spirit, the same way it did in high school around prom. Billy doesn't want James to even think he has a chance to have Malika.

He's willing to use his daughter to keep Malika from moving on. His daughter's love for him will keep her in his web.

London and Malika enter the house. London snatches her hand back angrily and slams her bedroom door. Surprised by London's rude behavior, Malika remarks, "That doesn't happen often. You better calm down little girl." Malika walks over to Noel who is fast asleep and nudges her awake.

"Wake up. Who is babysiting whom?"

Noel gets up and rubs her eyes. She takes a moment to gather her bearings and asks, "What?"

"London! She just ran outside while you were sleeping."

"I thought she was sleeping."

"I guess not," Malika says sarcastically.

"What happened, is she okay?"

"Yea. She just saw Billy and me arguing." Malika paces the room as Noel listens intently.

"What!? How did she know he was even there?"

"I think she looked through her window and

saw me arguing with him."

"You okay?" Noel says with concern.

"Yea. But I might have ruined everything with James. Billy is the same guy I dated after we broke up as kids. I hadn't told him that he's also London's father. He found out tonight when he dropped me off."

"Let me make us some coffee," Noel suggests, seeing that she won't be going to sleep anytime soon. Malika appreciates the gesture and nods her head in approval. Noel walks over to the kitchen to brew the coffee. "I have a lot to think about."

"Do you?" Noel says with a hint of sassiness, believing the answer to be clear.

Malika senses the disagreement in her tone and says, "Yea. Billy came here wanting me back." Malika listens to the coffee being brewed. Noel looks over to Malika to make sure she is heard as she speaks, "I know this is not my business, but as your friend, I would not be doing you any favors if I didn't take the time to tell you my opinion."

"Noel, you have never been the kind of friend who would hold back their opinion. What's up?"

Noel walks over to Malika and hands her a mug. She sits down on the couch next to Malika and says, "I know you don't want to hear this but let me say this before I leave, I just want you to listen."

"I'm listening."

Malika stops waltzing through the room and sits down on the couch next to Noel. Noel takes a moment and says, "I've seen you make the same decision over and over. I think you expect different results even after doing the same thing. For the life of me, I just don't get it. You always chose anyone other than James. Look how it has worked out so far. Somehow, you're both connected, and yet you still never take the chance to find out what's possible. We know that Billy is going to do what he always does - put himself first!

You choose Billy repeatedly. You know the result of him being in and out of your life. Do you need it to be the story of London's life too? To be waiting for a father who will always fall short when you need him most? Or do you take a chance on the guy that is willing to embrace you and your situation with no drawbacks? He wanted to be with you even after the mess you two were in as seventeen-year-olds?

My point is to give something else a chance. If you are getting back with him so London can have her father. That will be short-lived. At the end of the day, it's something for you to think about. I love you. And if you need me to babysit London so you can go on another date with James or someone else, I'll be here. But what I'll never support is you and Billy getting back together. I'll be happy to do so for anyone else. I love you."

Malika smiles and hugs Noel, "Thank you."

"Don't thank me and then ignore my advice. Let me get out of here. It's getting late." Noel rises from her seat on the couch and walks towards the door. Malika follows her to the door, hugs her while thanking her for babysitting. Noel looks at Malika and smiles. She opens the door and leaves. Malika tilts her head back and gazes at the ceiling as she closes the door. She takes a deep breath in and a deeper breath out…

Early morning on the next day, London walks out of her bedroom and onto the couch where Malika sleeps, drool coming down the side of her mouth.

"Mom? Mom? Are you awake?" Malika answers London with her eyes still closed. "I am now. Is everything okay?"

"Why were you mad at me when I saw Daddy? I just wanted to say hi."

Malika thinks briefly about the answer to London's question. "Well, the relationship between your dad and me is a bit complicated."

"How?"

"Your father and I argue a lot, and it got to a point where it wasn't good for either of us to be around that."

"How come he wanted to see you?"

"He said he wanted us to be a family, but that's not always an easy decision."

"Do you want us to be a family?"

"I do. Just not the way he wants us to be a family." London becomes visibly confused and stays silent. She waits for her mother to clarify in a way that she can understand.

"I want to be a family. Just not the way your father wants us to be a family. Your father wants me to date him so he can be the father that he is supposed to be to you. I want your dad in your life. However, he's showed me through his actions that he will always disappoint you. I don't want that to be the story of your childhood the way it was for mine. If you want to see daddy, I won't stand in the way. I'm not going to be with him though, and that is something that he wants. Just remember that he will always be your father, and you two can have a relationship without me. Does that make sense to you?"

"I guess. Can I call dad?"

"Yes. He said he was going to come by today, but you can call him. My cell phone is in my pocketbook"

Malika points to where her pocketbook is, and London runs over to take the phone out. Malika smiles that her daughter still makes her excited and prays that she doesn't continue to disappoint her little girl.

That evening London and Malika sit on the couch when they hear a knock on the door. London runs over and opens the door to see her father standing there with a teddy bear. Billy hands his gift to London, "Hey, baby girl."

London smiles as she's lifted into the air by Billy, "Hey, daddy."

Billy walks into the apartment. "Let me talk to your mother for a second sweetie."

Upon hearing this, Malika grabs her purse, stuffs her keys inside, and says to Billy as she walks towards the door, "We can talk when I come back."

Billy walks closer to Malika and whispers, "I'm here to fix us."

"There's nothing for you to fix, but it's always good to spend quality time with your daughter. I have to go out and make something right. I'll be back in a few hours."

Malika kisses her daughter and says, "Spend some time with daddy. I'll be back okay." London, excited to have some father-daughter time, says, "Okay."

"Daddy, I want you to see my new room. Then we can watch a movie." Billy takes a deep breath then chuckles. "Sure, let's see what your mother did to your room."

Billy walks with London into her bedroom. Malika smiles as she opens the front door and leaves the apartment…

LAW OF INSPIRED ACTION

Malika found out earlier in the evening that James was planning on eating dinner with his sister and nephew. She asked Jasmine if she would mind her coming by for a minute to speak to James.

Jasmine excited about the possibility of Malika and James dating says, "No! Not at all. In fact, bring along London as well.

Although Malika didn't explain the reason for her visit to Jasmine, she drives nervously over to the house. She finds herself driving as if she is taking the DMV exam - hands firmly placed at ten to two, eyes scanning her mirrors frequently like a paranoid person. She turns onto the block and gazes at her childhood home as she parks the car. Inside the Rose family home, James, Jasmine, and Adam are eating dinner when they hear a knock at the door.

Jasmine, knowing it to be Malika, smiles and says to Adam, "Hey check out who's at the door." Adam gets up from the dinner table and opens the door to see Malika standing on the other side, fully dressed up. She gives Adam a big smile as he steps aside to let Malika walk into the house.

"Hi miss Malika."

"Hey Adam, is your uncle here?" Adam points to James and goes back to his seat to finish his dinner. James sees Malika, excuses himself from the table, and walks over to the door.

James stands beside Malika, folding his arms to indicate his lack of interest in what Malika wants to tell him. He speaks in a careless tone to emphasize that he is unbothered by last night's events. "What's up?"

Malika, noticing his tone and not wanting to create a spectacle in front of his family, asks James if they can talk outside. James shrugs his shoulders, "I guess so." James steps outside with Malika. They both sit on the steps of the house.

"So..." Malika begins.

James looks out to the street and avoids making eye contact with Malika. He says, "If you are here to say something about last night. You don't need to."

"Yes. I do." James turns around to see Malika's eyes filled with sadness over him trying to be the bigger person, despite the fact that the entire situation was a disaster. Malika grabs James' hand and tries to hold it but he resists and withdraws it.

"Okay. I never thought I would have a chance to ever get back to you. Especially after the way you looked at me when you drove away on prom night. I was hoping to see you there and you never showed up. I chalked it up to us being kids. More time went by and I thought Billy was serious about me, but as it turns out I was just one of his many options. I ended up pregnant with London. I realized I could not go through the abortion process again. I remembered how I felt when I made the decision about our baby, and I just could not do it again. I tried to explain that to Billy, but he didn't care."

Malika cries. She wipes her eyes and takes a deep breath. "What I'm trying to say is that I'm sorry for upsetting you last night. Before that, the evening was one of the greatest in my life. I'm sorry for hurting you, and if you can ever forgive me, please do. Last night was awesome and I would love to see where this can go since we're both adults now. I would like to think that I know myself a lot better than when we were younger. Another reason why I feel stuck is that I would like for London to know her father. Even though I don't need anything to do with him, I know he wants the opposite. I want to move forward and maybe go on another date with you, but I need you to know that I cannot remove Billy from my life completely. My daughter deserves the opportunity to try and get to know her father.

I admit you are just as amazing now as you were when we were kids. We should have tried to figure it out. I'm sorry it took me seeing you after so many years and reminiscing down memory lane for me to realize that. Can you give me another chance?

James, maintaining a poker face, says, "Walk with me?"

"To where?"

James points at the basketball court where they had their first kiss. They both walk over holding each other's hands. Once at the basketball hoop, they embrace one another and share an everlasting kiss. They both smile after the kiss and hug one another as if neither one of them wanted to be the first one to let go…

James notices that Malika is a bit chilly and suggests that she should go back home to London. "Let's talk more tomorrow."

Malika on cloud nine smiles and says, "Yea. I should do that." James walks a few steps with Malika to her car.

She drives five minutes up the road to her apartment and enters. Billy and London are perched up on the couch watching a Disney movie. Billy sees that she is filled with energy and optimism. He glances at her dress and connects the dots. "You came back pretty fast. Where did you go?"

"It's nothing for you to worry about."

"What do you mean it's nothing for me to be worried about? He can't protect you or London. Not the way I can."

Malika sees the nervousness on London's face growing. Malika looks at her softly and says, "Hey baby, go inside your room. This will just take a minute."

London sprints into her room as she hates seeing her mother and father fight. As soon as the door closes Billy's tone heightens. "Who the hell do you think you are? Talking to me like that? How dare you try to embarrass me in front of London."

"Whatever. You need to go!"

"I'm not going anywhere until we settle this. I'm not coming back to save you from him breaking your heart."

"He never broke my heart, I broke his."

"Whatever," Billy says disgustedly.

"The only heart that matters is our daughter's. That is your obligation. Not trying to get us back together. That ship sailed a long time ago because of you. I need you to be a father now and be more present in London's life. I don't need you for me, but London loves you so please do better."

Billy smiles and snatches at Malika's hand, "You and London are a package deal. You want me to be there for her? I need you to be with me. That's the only way this is going to work, at least for me." London who has had her ear to her bedroom door the entire time hears her father's true feelings, opens her door abruptly, and runs out of the home.

Malika pulls her hand away from Billy and says, "Get out of my home. I now have to make an excuse for what she's just heard you say. You have to stop continuously breaking her heart." Malika rushes for the door when Billy yells, "So this is it? Huh, Malika?"

"The only thing I want is what I have been saying. Be the man you always said you wanted to be for your daughter. Also, claim some of your other kids and be the father figure you wish you had growing up.

Malika opens the door and finds London in the park around the building complex. She's rocking herself back and forth on the swing. Malika walks up and takes a seat on the swing next to her. London asks, "Did he leave yet?"

"He'll be gone by the time we get back to the apartment."

"I just don't know what I did for him to not want to spend time with me."

"He wants to be with you, but he also wants more than that. He didn't mean anything by our conversation. He just has some issues that he needs to work on by himself. It has nothing to do with you. Come on let's go back inside now. It's pretty cold out." Malika and London leave the park and walk back to their apartment...

James and Malika are on their second date when he decides to do something, he always wished they could do as kids - ice skating. James holds Malika's hand as they skate the large loop, both a tad nervous that they might are focused much more on the ice than on one another.

"So how's London doing?"

"She's okay. She's been a little melancholy

lately."

"Really? How come?"

James decides to skate backward so he can focus on her lips. The music through the speakers is playing too loudly for any meaningful conversation to take place, and he doesn't want to miss anything important.

"London is disappointed that she saw her father's true colors. She overheard us arguing. In summary, he wanted us to be an item in return for quality time with London."

James turns back around so he can skate in the same direction as Malika. "I'm sorry to hear that."

"Yeah, me too."

After the date, James drives Malika home. Before he heads home, he has the sudden urge to confront his supposed childhood arch-nemesis. James decides to put this to rest once and for all. He drives down the block he grew up on and knocks on Billy's front door.

James blows hot air from his mouth onto his hands to warm them as he waits for someone to open the door. James hears the sound of someone coming up or going down a flight of stairs, as the door finally opens. Billy sees that it's James and rolls his eyes, "What do you want? Give me one reason why I shouldn't beat your ass right now."

"Because I'll put you down before you could. Listen, I'm not here to fight you. I just want to let you know that I'm not trying to get in the way of you and your family. So all that bull you're trying to pull with Malika? Check it at the door and be there for London."

You don't know a thing about my daughter so stay the hell out of my family's business."

"I'm going to see Malika because that is what she and I want, but I'll never get in the way of you and your daughter. I don't know why you feel the way you do about me, but you got something more important to take care of."

"Oh yea, then what's that?"

"Your responsibilities. I'm not your problem, and neither is London. Your problem is within yourself. London is a sweet girl that just wants her father to show a little interest. I'm not a parent but I know it's a full-time job. Malika is only asking for you to be present in something you two created." Billy says nothing as James leaves the premises, goes back into his car, and drives home…

THE UNIVERSE

Months into dating James, Malika has just finished watching a movie chosen by London. After the movie, James begins to clean up the Chinese food that they had eaten. London, curious to know more about James and her mother when they were kids, asks, "Did you guys eat a lot of Chinese food growing up?" James assesses the question and says to London, "I can't say that we did, why?" "You and mom order the same thing. Almost like you guys are the same person." James smiles at London appreciating the compliment if it was meant to be one. He smiles at London and looks at Malika. Malika gets up from the couch and helps James in putting away the silverware and plates into the sink. She adds to London and James' conversation, "I think I can answer that. Once a month I would go over to his parents' house and have Chinese food. I would always eat whatever he asked his parents to order. It's never changed. It's always been pork-fried rice and sesame chicken. James smiles and hugs Malika as London look at them get all mushy in

the kitchen.
"What can I say I'm a creature of old habits." James remarks.
Malika smiles as they hug one another closer. London sees this and closes her eyes. "Okay. I get it. I get it. That's enough PDA for today you two." London hoping that they would stop what just happened walks out of the room and into her bedroom. James and Malika laugh as London exits. "How does she know what PDA is?" James says with a smile, in awe of her knowledge at such a young age.

"I want to say either social media or YouTube. She is too smart for her own good."

"She's hilarious."

"Yea she is. That's my girl."

"Is London okay with us being with one another?"

"She likes you. I think she is cautious because the only other man that's been in her life was Billy. He was not as attentive as he should have been as a father. I think she might be afraid to get so attached in case we don't work out."

"We have been together for some time now. I would like to do something nice for your daughter. Is that okay with you? I'll bring my nephew, Adam. They can have a play date. What do you think?"

"I think that'll be cool. I can catch up with Jasmine while you take the kids."

"Sounds good. I'll set it up for some time next week.

Malika not wanting him to feel like there's a rush, verifies, "You sure?"

James, not seeing the problem, shrugs his shoulders, "Yea why not? I'm sure my sister can use some help with Adam, and I know how busy you are with London. I'll make sure they have fun."

"You're probably right. Just let me see how Jasmine feels about all this. I'm fine with it. I'll also have to see what London thinks."

"That's all good. I'll check with my sister and let you know." James hugs Malika as he grabs his spring coat and walks out of the house. Malika smiles and they decide to speak tomorrow.

James walks out of Malika's apartment, at peace with his life. London comes out of her bedroom as she hears the door closing. London asks, "James left already?"

"He did but he wanted to know if you wanted to hang out with him and Adam sometime next week. He will probably take you guys to the park to do something fun. Are you up for that?"

"London excited to have something to do says, "Yes."

"Okay. I'll let him know tomorrow. It's getting late. Wash up and get ready for bed."

London leaves the room and goes into the bathroom to wash up and get ready for bed…

Jasmine and Adam are at home eating dinner with her parents. They've just returned from their vacation. "Mom, this food looks delicious."

"You know I just had to cook a big meal for my baby."

Jasmine blushes at the fact that her mom still treats her as if she's twelve. "Thanks, mom. Adam and I appreciate it."

"I didn't mean you. I'm talking about James. He's still coming over, right?"

Patricia, Jim, and Adam smile at one another and then look at Jasmine. She rolls her eyes over the favoritism that James receives. They try to hold in their laughs but can't help themselves.

"Very funny," Jasmine says sarcastically.

"Is uncle James coming?" Adam inquires, hoping to see his uncle.

"He said he'll be here."

Adam hoping to hang out with someone his age asks if London and Malika will be with him.

Patricia is shocked as she remembers the sweet teenage love between the two. She looks at Adam with surprise.

"Malika? Malika? And who's London?" Adam looks for Jasmine to answer the question. Jasmine smiles and hides her lips, indicating that she will say nothing and has no idea what the answer is.

Jasmine, Malika, Patricia, and Adam hear a knock at the front door. Adam gets up from his seat and walks towards the door and opens it.

"Hey, Uncle James," he says with excitement.

James looks at Adam gives him big hug. "What's up? How are you doing?

"Pretty good. We've been waiting for you, so we can eat."

James and Adam walk to the table to have a seat. He gives his dad a hug and a kiss to his mom before he seats himself.

"Hey, sweetie."

"Hey, mom. What's up family?"

The family puts food on their plates besides James. "Wow. Mom all this looks delicious." James says to his mom.

"Then why is there none on your plate. How have you been?"

"I just ate with Malika and London. I've been

good. Can't really complain. Just been really busy with my businesses."

Jim sees an opportunity and comments, "You're sure it's not Malika that has made everything feel good." James looks at his family blankly. His parents smile. "I see that my sister and nephew could not keep their mouths quiet," James says while looking at Adam and Jasmine.

"You two are dating again? Who's London?"

"Yea we have been seeing one other for a few months. London is her daughter."

"Well, how are things going?" Patricia asks James.

"I don't feel like it's something to be talked about while there are kids in the room"

Adam pouts and gets up off his seat. "Not you, Adam. I'm talking about your mother." James laughs.

Jasmine tells James to shut up. Jim looks at Jasmine and says, "You heard your brother."

"Yea, we want to hear this," Patricia tells Adam and Jasmine to step out of the room. Jasmine taps Adam on his shoulder. They grab their plates and walk out of the room and into Jasmines' bedroom to continue eating.
Jim casts a glance and waits for their door to close. "Okay. They're gone."

Patricia asks, "How come you didn't tell me that you and Malika were back together? You know I always thought you two were so good for each other."

"That's true. Your mother would have a thousand and one questions on why you two were no longer together. Asking me as if you ever came to me for advice."

Jim chuckles as he reminisces over how much Patricia had wanted that relationship to work.

"Well, no need to ask now. How are you two doing?"

"Good. Great! I want to ask her daughter if she is okay with me asking Malika to marry me."

"That's a big step. I know you would make a great husband. She has always been a lovely lady. Nothing would make me happier than you guys together." Patricia says.

"Thanks. It's very early but when you know you know."

Jim looks at his son knowingly. "I can understand that. I think we should talk."

Jim asks Patricia to excuse them so he can have some alone time with his son. Jim walks into the kitchen and makes a drink for the two men.

Jim brings the cocktails back to the dining

room table where they both take a sip before going out to the backyard to speak openly but privately.

"So what's up pops?" James asks.

"I just wanted to enjoy the fresh air with you."

"Okay."

James takes a deep breath and takes in the scenery.

"You've to be happy at the end of the day." Jim says, finally breaking the silence.

"What do you mean? I'm happy."

"What I'm saying is, don't let your mother or me dictate a situation for you. Your mom likes Malika and that's great. So do I. However, if there are issues that are truly unresolved from when you were children, they'll follow you two into adulthood. Do what you feel is right. If you approve of her yourself and the way she makes you feel, nothing else matters.

"Thanks for the talk."

James gives a slight smile to Jim. Jim taps his son's shoulder and walks back inside. James takes a sip of his drink and turns his head to the house that Malika grew up in. He understands why his father wanted to pull him away and make sure that any decision made is truly his and not for the excitement or wants of others…

The next week James stands with Adam outside Malika's apartment. James knocks on the door. Malika walks to the door and opens it wide. "London is almost ready. You guys come on in." James and Adam walk into the apartment. James gives Malika a peck on the lips. Adam observant of how well the house has been kept together says, "You have a nice home. Miss Malika."

Malika smiles, appreciates the compliment from James, and says, "Oh well thank you, Adam." "Hey, where are you taking them?" Malika asks James. James informs her of his plan to take the kids to the small amusement park around town.

Malika smiles and nods her head in approval, knowing that London will be excited about the things that James has planned.

London enters the living room and says, "I'm ready."

"Perfect. Come on, guys." Malika says as she hugs London. "You guys have fun." James smiles at Malika as he opens the door for London and Adam to leave the apartment.

"They will. I'll make sure of it," Says James

At the park, the kids weave in and out of

conversation as they run through the amusement park rides. James gets the kids on the largest roller coaster there, smiling as they go up and down the roller coaster. The sight of them having so much fun just being kids brings great joy to him.

After the fun rides at the park, each of them looks through the food trucks in search of something they'd like. They finally settle on Nathan's hotdog stand.

London says to Adam and James, "I think we should have gone on a few more rides before eating."

"Sorry buddy," Replies James.

"It's okay. I don't feel so good. I'll be right back." Adam runs away from London and James to go on another ride.

"Are you having a good time?"

London looks at James to answer, "Yea, it's been a lot of fun."

"Can I ask you something?"

"Yes?"

James takes a deep breath as one does before speaking to a parent. He would love for London to give him her blessings to marry her mom. "Do you like me hanging with your mom?" he finally manages to say.

"Yea, I guess you make her happy and you

seem to be pretty cool." James smiles, excited to be viewed as cool. "I want make her even happier, but I need your permission first."

"My permission? For what?" London responds with an inquisitive look on her face.

"I want your permission to marry you mom, and perhaps be a part of your family." London gazes at James before she speaks.

"Let me think about it, James." James becomes dejected. Unsure what her answer would be, he smiles and says, "Of course, yea take your time."

London smiles, lets out a chuckle then says, "I'm joking, James. Yes! It's okay."

"You had me there for a second," James says as they both laugh.

"I know. Though I'm curious, when do you want to ask my mom to marry you?"

"I was hoping you could help me with that."

"Really?"

"Yea," responds James.

"What do you have in mind?"

James and London go through a few ideas to make sure that the engagement goes well. As they go back and forth, they plan out how James will present the ring.

Two weeks after James got permission from London to marry her mom, the three of them rode their bikes through town to the dream home that James just bought. The same house that he and Malika wished for when they were seventeen.

They make it to the other side of town, populated by other beautiful homes. They all get off their bikes and look out to the water, where boats move around peacefully.

James says to Malika, "You remember this house."

"How can I forget?" London goes into her pocket, takes out a small ring box, and hands it to James. James gets on one knee. "I know we're no longer kids, but whenever we spend time together I still get the same butterflies as I did when we were kids. I would love to feel this way forever." He pauses for a moment, and says, "Malika, will you marry me?"
Malika gives out a wide smile. She looks at her daughter to see her smiling and nodding in agreement. "Say yes!" London whispers to her.

Malika shakes with excitement and yells, "Yes! Of course, I'll marry you."

James slides the ring onto her ring finger, gets off the ground, and kisses Malika. London is happy to see her mom radiating with joy…

In the same way as the universe works to

fulfill our desires for more money, a house, or a car, it also works when it comes to true love. What might appear to have been lost forever may not be so lost after all.

A wise man once said, "If you love something let it go. If it comes back to you, it's yours forever. If it doesn't, then it was never meant to be." Never meant to be is the story for many but a lucky few get the chance to reconnect with those that meant the world to them as a kid.

Whether that's just for closure, so you can move forward, or a sign to pick up where you left off, never fight the universe. The universe knows what's best. The universe loves you, even when you think it has stopped looking out for you.

The love that the universe has for us, protects us from things we may never see coming or prepares us for something better. Who are we to ever question it? After all, the universe is the adult and we're just the kids...

ABOUT THE AUTHOR

Brinton was born in the Bronx, New York and raised in the greater New York area. He enrolled at New England College, completing his degree in three years. Brinton received his Bachelor of Arts degree in Business Administration with a minor in Sociology in 2011. With a passion for expressing his life through words in order to touch the lives of others, His debut book, **The Dreamer: The Boy Who Caught 22** was released in January 2014.

Cancer & the Lottery was released in 2015 and **Cancer & the Lottery Ally's way** in 2016. **Hometown Heroes** 2016. **The Tailor in Heaven** 2019. **Noah Moss the Chef** 2020.

Kids of the Diaspora 2020. **A Love in Central Park** 2021. **Kids of the Diaspora: The Black Kid Manifesto**

Books can be purchased from Amazon.com

Made in the USA
Middletown, DE
10 July 2021

43914727R00089